BLOOD AND GEARS

Declan Cosson

CONTENTS

"Their business is war and they do their business".
-Rudyard Kipling

"It was not the end...nor the beginning of the end...but the end of the beginning."
-Winston Churchill

"And moving at unheard commands,

The abysses and vast fires between,

Flit figures that, with clanking hands,

Obey a hideous routine.

They are not flesh, they are not bone,

They see not with the human eye,

And from their iron lips is blown

A dreadful and monotonous cry."

-Archibald Lampman

PROLOGUE

The main military of mankind in the mid-24th century, the Legion was an elite force that had its origins in World War 3. By the middle of the 21st century, humanity had reached a second *Belle Epoque*. Innovations such as nuclear fusion, replication of metals and hydrogen fuel cells had freed mankind from fossil fuels, while allowing for the construction of enormous vehicles and projects that humanity in previous centuries could only dream of. Economies grew stronger and the rate of homelessness and poverty dramatically decreased.

However, the mid-21st century and 22nd century also saw a decline in the power of America and the rise of other great powers such as Russia, China, Greater Albion (comprised of Great Britain, Australia, Canada and New Zealand) and the United States of Europe. Each of these powers had more efficient economies and stronger armies than America. Other prominent powers that rose included Japan, South Africa and Brazil, all trying to assert themselves in this new fossil fuel free age. However, a power struggle emerged between the five great powers of China, Russia, America, Greater Albion and Europe culminating in the declaration of war. This new Third World War dragged almost every single country in the world into its chaos.

During this global struggle, all four armies of the Great Powers were locked in competition to produce powerful high-quality infantry that could win battles with as few casualties as possible. While the other three factions focused on building robotic soldiers, Europe and Greater Albion worked together and went down a different path by experimenting with the "Legionnaire Programme", a project focused around modifying young men into super soldiers that became known as Legionnaires.

These men would be put through a gruelling training process that would forge them into battle-hardened infantry that could take on almost anything. The robotic armies, while powerful rivals, had no conscience implanted in them. As a result, they showed little teamwork or compassion for their victims, meaning that the robotic armies of the Great Powers committed more atrocities than all the armies of WW2 combined. The lack of conscience turned out to be a serious mistake for humanity as when China, in desperation to save its people from an American invasion, unleashed the Black Mouth, a giant metallic monster that could control enemy robots.

However, the Black Mouth had no conscience and turned on its people and began its own war in consequence. In this war, the great powers of Russia, China and the US fell to the rebelling robots. Most of mankind banded together using old weapons from the early 21st century to try to fight back while their governments were thrown into disarray. It was at this moment that Europe and Greater Albion fused into one single nation, an empire comprised of self-ruling regions. Having restructured its doctrines, this new nation sent out its legionnaires, who were originally just defending Europe, to help support what remained of civilisation. What began was a gruelling perpetual war against the machines. Mankind was united under one government called "Terra" (meaning Earth in Latin). Though centred in London, Terra divided the world into administrative zones that would be focused on ruling their region and preserving its own respective culture as well as developing the region's infrastructure.

It is now the 24th century: The Legion became the official army of humanity in its war against the machines and its war to defend and reclaim the civilised world from the iron fist of the machine is far from over.

CHAPTER 1: A DAY IN THE LEGION

It was the year 2356: The clouds were as thick as the waters of an ocean, shielding the ground below from the light of the sun. At that moment, it seemed quiet. Then a loud noise could be heard in the distance: the sound of many jet engines. Any bird that was migrating immediately fluttered away at the sound of the noise as it got louder and louder while a vast shape burst through the clouds. Coming forward was a vessel that looked to be a cross between an aircraft carrier and a battleship. Keeping the enormous craft airborne were 12 engines, 6 on either side. There were six engines at the front, three on either side and six engines at the back, with, similarly, three on either side. All of these engines were powered by a fusion core which was at the centre of the ship.

The ship was bristling with a wide array of heavy weapons, missile launchers and miniguns. Hanging from below the vessel were an array of giant guns with three barrels each. At the centre of the craft was a control tower that had a complicated array of antennas and a satellite dish; etched on the side of the vessel was the name *Tungsten*. This was a flying fortress.

In the command centre, pilots, dressed in dark green uniforms and peakless caps, were operating the controls and observing the radars while a troop of officers were observing a holographic map. The officers also had smart uniforms, but they wore visored peaked caps instead. Depicted on the map was the battlefield that they were heading to. There were two sides to the map, green and red. Green stood for humanity and red stood for the machines. This time, the red was expanding rapidly over the battlefield. This was a sign that the army that was fighting to defend Edinburgh was on the verge of total collapse. The main officer, Rufus Thorne, stared at the map for a long time. Thorne had a tall imposing body and a pale but aquiline shaped beardless face that made him look similar to figures such as Julius Caesar.

Coming up behind Thorne was another pale skinned officer, although he had white hair and a shaved but rugged face.

"Commander Thorne, sir?" He said to Rufus.

Turning around, Thorne replied, "Colonel Jethro, the battle is going ill, this seems to happen whenever we don't have a flying fortress in the area! Tell the men to prepare the guns for bombardment!"

However just as Rufus gave that order, another officer said, "Sir, that may not be an option. At least not just now!"

Turning around, Rufus asked, "What? What is the situation? Explain yourself, James!"

As he examined the holographic map, James said to Rufus, "Sir, I can detect multiple armoured SAM vehicles on the battlefield. A single SAM tank would be enough to pulverise even the toughest flying fortress. Any heavy dropship carrying armoured divisions and regular battalions would be cooked as well!"

Rufus walked over to the holographic map and saw the machines James was talking about. He asked, "What about flacks? These SAMs aren't so good against cloaked and smaller aircraft!"

"Flak and light missile bots are moving to support the backbone infantry, making any form of close air support against the horde to be ineffective and suicidal, sir! But a small dropship can make it to the SAMs if it stays above the clouds, but I would warn you, sir, a pack of such vessels would generate enough mass for the SAMs to knock them all out of the sky at once!"

Observing the map for a prolonged period, Rufus then stood up and said to James, "Thank you for the advice, James! A single small dropship should be able to do the job." Before turning around to Jethro and saying, "Colonel Jethro, contact Alpha Squad, tell them that they are to strike the SAMs!"

"Yes sir! I will alert Captain Michael T. Faulkner that his squad is to be at the ready!"

Meanwhile at the bar, a pool game was going on between two men, one slim with pale skin, green eyes and light brown hair and the other with a stronger, bulkier body and dark skin. The slim man was on a streak, having just potted his third ball. His stick struck the white ball, sending it hurtling into a striped ball causing it to tumble into a hole. The darker skinned man laughed as he said

"Damn it, Dermot, whenever I play you, you always win!"

"Aye, indeed, Dia, that is why you don't play a sniper; training and constant practice has led my eyes to be as sharp as a hawk. They need to be sharp if I'm going to snipe!"

"That is true, man, and I thank my ancestors that we have you every day. You've saved our lives numerous times, Dermot."

"Ah yeah, but I'm doing my job! Besides, you're doing better at pool than you did when we first played! After all, you saved my life more times than I can count."

The two laughed as Dia finally got a chance to pot a ball. Another two men were playing darts. Both of them were strong and hefty, one was paler than the other and had dark brown hair while the other had brown skin and had his body patterned with Māori tattoos. Both of them were goofing while flinging darts. One of them said to the other, "So, Vincent? I hear we are approaching the city of Edinburgh today."

"I know Hans, yet another job at the front. It's what our life has been about, just killing and dying."

"We are putting our lives on the line for the state of Terra, Vincent. Don't you have some pride in our nation? There are not many nations that could have resisted an army like that of the machines. It is a nation favoured by God!"

"For the sake of Terran values, Terran law and Terran morality! Eh, I couldn't care less about the suits in Westminster, those suits always expect us troopers to be on the best of our behaviour while they bicker like five-year-olds. No wonder Commander Thorne is always in a bad mood after he comes back from London! After all, it was the suits who made those machines in the first place, and what else do you get when you programme something to just kill? You get a batch of metallic psychopaths!! If God actually existed, he would have put an end to this nonsense!!"

"Vincent, as annoying as the politicians may be, they are the ones whose decisions are holding our society together. They are as frustrated by this dreadful war as we are. The problem is, Vincent, the machines are not willing to talk or even consider peace, so we have no choice but to fight," Hans replied.

"That's right Hans, that's why nobody deserts their post here, we owe each other everything!"

"To think at one time, we had a large regiment, just like everyone else. Now, after the battle for Kyiv, we are only seven. I was nineteen when that happened."

"I know, Hans, you saved my life back then and Michael took charge. It's why I'll never forget that time."

Hans and Vincent gave each other a knuckle touch. It was a sign of their friendship, for the two had been inseparable since that battle on the outskirts of Kyiv.

Meanwhile Chang was sitting down, reading *The Art of War*. He read this book practically all the time whenever he was not on duty. He looked up to see a figure with tanned skin, clean-shaven with raven hair sitting at the counter. The man looked to be the very image of Lord Byron himself. Chang continued to read his book when another man who looked pale yet strong and athletic came over and asked

"Chang? What are you reading?"

"I am reading *The Art of War* Alexi. If you're looking for a book to read, then I'd be happy to share it with you."

Alexi chuckled as he said "You're always reading that book, Chang, as if you are in your own world, why don't you play with the rest of us?"

"This book tells many good techniques about war, Alexi, even the highest-ranking commanders in Terra use talents learned from this book. It is important for a warrior to read."

"Really Chang? Look at Dermot and Dia, they constantly play games like pool, I've rarely seen them pick up a book. Honestly, I put my trust in God when it comes to fighting."

"God? If that works for you, good to know. Me, I prefer to put my trust in plans and my own intuition. Which is better to put one's trust in, you might ask? That Alexi, we can find out with a game once we get the chance. How about that?"

Alexi smirked. The group continued to have their fun while

the Byronic figure sat at the counter. As he heard the laughter of the team, the barkeep asked his raven-haired customer

"Aren't you going to join them, Michael?"

"I can't afford to let my guard down. Jethro could call us at any minute, we are approaching the city of Edinburgh."

Michael observed his group as they had their fun. Looking at his watch, he knew that the flying fortress would be over Edinburg soon, it would be the first of the fleet to show up.

Michael suddenly heard a beeping noise in his pocket. He pulled his communicator, a small radio that he carried at all times, from his pocket. Pressing it to his ear he asked, "Yes, sir, this is Captain Faulkner, over."

"Captain Faulkner, we need your team to be ready right now! We have discovered SAM tanks in Edinburgh, enough to pulverise a flying fortress meaning that our boys on the ground won't have air support unless you and your team take them out! Over!"

"Understood, we won't let you down, sir! Over and out!"

Michael put the communicator back into his pocket and announced to the team

"Gentlemen! We've got orders from Jethro and Rufus Thorne! Head to the armoury!"

At the sound of this, the team immediately stopped what they were doing and rushed to the armoury to suit up.

***

Meanwhile, back up in the control tower, Jethro said to Rufus, "Sir! Alpha Squad is heading out to suit up! They will soon be ready!"

"Good, inform the other Legions to deploy! I want their dropships to be ready to debark the moment I give the order! Is that understood?"

"Yes, sir!"

And with that, the order was relayed to all the Legionnaires in the *Tungsten* to prepare for battle.

❋ ❋ ❋

As the alarms sounded through the flying fortress, the seven members of Alpha Squad: Michael, Dia, Chang, Vincent, Alexi, Hans and Dermot were already in the armoury where the rest of the men were headed. Most of the men wore dark brown uniforms, over which they fitted armour coloured dark green and made of steel. This armour comprised breastplates, shin guards, boots and steel helmets. They also wore gloves and boots to keep them warm. The helmets were semi-spherical, with a chinstrap underneath. Covering their faces were gas masks. The masks had a transparent visor so that the soldier could see what he was doing.

Hans and Vincent however, pulled on heavier armour than the others. It was so heavy that they needed engineers to help them. Their armour paralleled some sort of space suit and it was powered by an electric engine. Patterned on their armour were both the symbol of the Orca as well as the initial A to symbolise they are part of Alpha Squad. All the members of Alpha Squad had the symbol of an Orca etched on their gear and they were known to the other units as 'Team Orca'. Their helmets and breastplates all had individual symbols on them: Michael had a wolf, symbolic of his status as the Alpha of the team. Chang had a panther, a symbol of intelligence and careful planning. Alexi had a shark while Dia had a lion etched on his. In Terra, both the lion and the shark symbolised determination regardless of the situation.

Dermot had a much sleeker outfit and had a baseball cap with headphones to protect his ears. Patterned on his shoulder was the image of a serpent. In Terra, the serpent was the symbol of stealth, fitting Dermot's position as a sniper. Added to his backpack was a medical kit, meaning that as well as being the team's sniper, he was their medic too.

Once suited up, they proceeded to the weapons storage where they got their assault rifles, snipers, miniguns, rocket launchers and flamethrowers. Since they were up against robots, every Legionnaire's weaponry had armour piercing bullets. Loudspeakers told the troops to head for the hangers and get to their dropships. Regardless of rank, they barely had any time to think as they rushed through the corridors of the flying fortress towards the hangar. Some of the younger ones took out their flasks to gorge on fresh icy water so that they could hydrate themselves before the oncoming fight. Others quickly blessed themselves as they knew that it could be their last battle.

Even before the men got there, the hangars were already full of activity as the ground crews were preparing aircraft for take-off. Arrayed in a disciplined line were the dropships. The dropships were essentially giant helicopter gunships with two hover jets on either side. They bristled with missiles and heavy machine guns. They had a cargo hull to store the troops, which they would transport from one location to another. Some of the biggest dropships were going to be transporting armoured vehicles such as tanks. Ground crew used hand signals to communicate to the crew within the vehicles so as to give them directions. The vehicles moved as slowly as possible up into the cargo bay of the dropships so as to avoid accident. The troops of Legionnaires entered the hangar, being directed by officers to their respective dropships.

Meanwhile as they got up the ramp of their dropship, Hans asked Vincent, "So, we are going to Edinburgh?"

"Yeah, not that it makes any difference...the code and practice will be the same as any other battle, keep as many new meats from dying on their first day alright...we just beat the shit out of any fucking machine in sight, alright?"

"I know the drill, Vincent...most important of all, we stay together!"

The two clanked their fists together, doing a knuckle touch before they boarded with the rest of Alpha Squad. Once the squad had entered the dropship, they found their pilot, Alonzo waiting for them. Marked on his shoulder pad was the symbol of a swan. Seeing them show up, Alonzo said with enthusiasm to Michael, "Captain Faulkner? Hello Amigos! What is it this time?"

"Good to see you, Alonzo! You need to fly us behind enemy lines!" Michael said, as Alonzo saluted him.

"Again? Really? Rufus seems to want you dead?"

"Yeah, well, we're elites, we have our own dropship and we have you! You can get us safely there, can't you?"

"Of course, I can! Checks have been completed, the hydrogen fuel cells have been filled up, everything is good to go!"

11

"Good, take her to Edinburgh, Alonzo!"

"Yes, sir! Come on Amigos! Buckle up and hang on tight!"

Once the team had buckled up, the dropship was towed out of the hangar. As they were elites, the seven members of Alpha Squad got a dropship to themselves to fly them to the battle. It was smaller and sleeker than the other dropships allowing it to be more agile.

CHAPTER 2: SIEGE OF EDINBURGH

Below the clouds, the castle that overlooked Edinburgh had become a tattered ruin as its once formidable walls stood no chance against the modern, missile-launching artillery of the machines. Still, its position on the high ground which overlooked the city gave an advantage to its defenders. These consisted both of the Home Guard garrison of Scotland and a Legionnaire unit which had been deployed in Edinburgh prior to the invasion. The ruined walls of the castle had been reinforced with entrenchments. Home Guardsmen were mortal soldiers, unlike their superhuman counterparts, the Legionnaires. As a result, despite being better armoured than the Legionnaires and well-armed, they died easily at the mercy of the machines.

However, that didn't stop them from putting up a grim and determined defence of their city. Very rarely did they retreat. Their goal was to defend populated areas while the Legionnaires spearheaded the counter attacks against the machines. Considering the Legionnaires had mechanised artillery and heavy tanks, that didn't seem like a bad idea. The problem was, the Legionnaires were being forced to halt and to entrench. This was because the machines were bombarding them with heavy artillery which was defended by SAMs. As a result, the battle had dragged into a stalemate. It was by the Museum of Edinburgh that the command vehicle was positioned. In the command vehicle, generals of the Home Guard, led by Field Commander McKee were planning their moves as they looked down at a holographic map. One of the generals asked his central commander:

"Commander McKee, there is only so much we can do. The machines have trapped us in a stalemate. Anything we send at them to breach their fortifications gets destroyed by their artillery. Already they are moving their largest guns in. We need to issue a retreat! Our men will be pulverised!"

"General O'Neill that is absolutely out of the question! Such a defeat would allow the North Sea machine detachment to punch through the North of England. Their guns would be capable of bombarding London. London is the centre of Terran authority, we cannot allow it to fall!" McKee said in reply.

"What are our orders, sir?"

McKee paused as he examined the holographic map. He was painfully aware that at this current moment, any form of aerial intervention would be knocked out of the sky by machine SAMs. But then he noticed a small blip flying across the city of Edinburgh.

He turned to O'Neill and said, "For now, we continue to dig in and repulse any machine attacks! A dropship seems to be flying in. Let us hope that Rufus Thorne has sent an ops team to deal with the machines."

* * *

Back up near the ruined walls of Edinburgh Castle, two Home Guardsmen were on the lookout from their trench. One of them was peering through his binoculars. Looking up, he saw what appeared to be a dropship. He nudged his comrade and said, "Hey, look up there? Do you see?"

"In the sky?"

"Yeah, it's a dropship, its small and it is on its own! And look!! It just went invisible!"

"So, they're banking their plans on a cloaked dropship! That's really encouraging!!"

"Not just any dropship, Laddie!! That's Good old Team Orca up there, not many are so stubbornly brave as to go in a single dropship right behind enemy lines!"

* * *

The dropship of Alpha Squad hovered over the battle. Alonzo kept it as high in the air as possible so as to avoid being shredded by the flaks below. During the rocky and bumpy voyage towards

Edinburgh, Michael had briefed his team

"Boys, these are the orders we got from Rufus Thorne....we will be heading for Edinburgh which has been taken by surprise by a machine army that was unleashed from their base in the North Sea. We will not be pulling in the flying fortresses just yet...we have word that the machines have just brought in heavy SAM tanks. Those bad boys are inefficient at hitting small targets but they can make quick work of a flying fortress if given the chance...this is why we have to take them out. Already a Legion is doing battle with the machines, but we will be behind enemy lines so until we can safely call in our air support...we'll be on our own! Any questions?"

Dermot spoke, asking, "Well, we've been on our own before sir, but what about the rest of the reinforcements? Aren't those boys going to have our backs?"

"No! Since their dropships are bigger, they'll be easier targets than we are, they'll come in when we've taken out as much anti-aircraft weaponry as possible...you know what to do now boys!"

"Yes, sir!"

* * *

Alonzo kept his calm as he desperately tried to manoeuvre the dropship as close as possible to the SAM tanks without getting hit. Once he maneuvered the dropship away from the SAMs, Alonzo landed the dropship onto the ground.

With the dropship firmly on the ground, the ramp came down and the squad ducked out of the vessel and immediately got to cover, kneeling in a circle to discuss their plan. They could hear thunder and gunfire in the distance. Michael then asked

"Hear that? That is the sound of our blokes doing battle in their trenches...they won't be able to stand for long because of the machine's heavy artillery. Taking out the artillery is normally the job of our air force, but they have the SAM tanks which can cleave through any flying fortress and bring it crashing into Edinburgh!"

"So, what's the idea? Let's get this over with!" Vincent asked.

"Aren't you interested in a good plan? Effective coordination of troops takes time you know!" Chang, known for his patient personality, replied.

Dia, who wanted to get into the heat of action as quickly as possible, snapped at Chang.
"Chang...we're not in the bar..."

"Silence! You three!" Michael shouted, knowing that a row would slow down the mission and sap precious time and effort. "Now is not the time for a petty argument," he continued, "... Vincent, you and Hans will be drawing the robotic garrison away from the SAMs, we need to isolate those machines if we are going to have any chance of taking them out. Chang, Dia, Alexi and I will be covering your advance with anti-tank equipment and you, Dermot...you will go up that chapel spire and snipe any targets that you see, do you get me, gentlemen?"

"We got you sir!" The team shouted in unison. Then they took their positions and waited for the enemy to come.

* * *

Meanwhile, in the control room of the flying fortress *Tungsten*, Thorne could see on the virtual map that things were getting worse for the army in Edinburgh. That being said, the green on the holographic map was starting to push forward, indicating that they were starting to fight back against the oncoming tide of machines. Rufus asked Jethro, "Report Colonel Jethro, what is the status of Alpha Squad?"

"They've already landed, sir, they will be making their way to the SAM tanks."

"And do they have a fixed plan on how they handle this!"

"I don't know...they often tend to make things up as they go along!"

"Oh God, let us pray that they know what they are doing."

Rufus continued to stare at the holographic map as he observed the battle. He was unable to take his mind off this map during the battle.

* * *

Down on the ground, two robotic sentries were guarding a SAM tank. It was a giant vehicle that had four pairs of tracks, two on either side of the front and two on either side of the back. It had been deployed so it had two pairs of missiles arching upwards. A robot was waiting on the deck of the tank, observing the skies with binoculars that could see through the clouds. If it saw a flying fortress coming into sight, it would fire one of the missiles. The two machine troopers guarding the tank had their weapons at the ready. The thundering orchestra of explosions from the battle could be heard from this distance. One of them asked, "What is going on out there?"

"Do not worry...the humans with their human emotions won't fight on for long once they realise that the battle isn't in their favour...even a Legion can be broken."

Suddenly a bullet fired from a chapel steeple shot through the head of one of the robots, causing it to shut down.

Confused, the other robot looked up and blazed its machine gun only to be shot in his turn. The bullet pierced straight through its chest, causing it to collapse to the ground. Dermot's sapphire eyes glared coldly as he reloaded his gun. He watched from the chapel steeple as the bots tried to organise themselves. Robotic soldiers readied themselves but then Vincent and Hans came with their armour piercing miniguns, wiping out all the robotic soldiers in sight. The two troopers knuckle touched again, but a sniper bullet bounced off Han's armour. Before they could react, Dermot sniped the drone responsible. With the area clear, Dia then fired a missile that took out the SAM tank. The group then rushed away from the vehicle as it blew up, knocking them to the ground. As the team started to get up, Chang remarked, "Well, that was too easy!! Surely something that could take down a flying fortress would receive more protection, wouldn't they?"

"Don't worry, we still have more SAM tanks to go!! Alexi responded. "Once the machines know that we are here, there should be more coming. Besides most of them are clearing out the last vestiges of the Edinburgh garrison, so let's take advantage of this! God is with us!"

Because most of the robots were fighting at the front, storming the trenches of the garrison, the SAM tanks were lightly guarded, meaning that for elite Legionnaires like those of the Alpha Squad, taking them out was business as usual. And for them, business was gritty, harsh and dirty. However, before they could take out the last one, a giant three-legged walker showed up bristling with missiles and machine guns. The team fired all that they had at the machine, but it barely scratched the giant monster.

Seeing that they were easily outmatched, Michael ordered them to take cover in a house and garrison it. From the house, the team continued to stand their ground. However, as the rest of the team took cover among the buildings, Hans continued to blaze his minigun. He wanted to distract the machine before it could turn around to decimate the house. Vincent called out to Hans, telling him to get into the house. Hans however stood his ground. Dermot tried sniping at the joints, but the bullets barely dented them. Seeing the SAM tank, which was still in position, Alexi fired at it with a rocket launcher, causing it to blow up. The walker then got into a rage and blazed it's miniguns, shredding through Hans and causing him to tumble.

"Hans! No! NO! NO!" Vincent yelled.

He ran out of the house towards a dying Hans. He stumbled down beside Hans, lifting his comrade's visor to see him coughing up blood. He dragged the dying Hans behind a van.

As Vincent clung onto him, Hans said, "Vincent, don't worry about me, I'm a goner, you're going to have to move on without me!!"

"No, don't you fucking dare call yourself a goner! You saved my life before, it's time I returned the favour. Mark me, Hans...you're going to live!"

"Damn it, Vincent, my body may be busted...but I'll always be there...even if you don't see me!"

Before Vincent could say anymore, the tripod turned its attention to them, blasting the van. Seeing this, Michael helped

Vincent drag Hans over into the house just as three more tripod tanks and countless robot soldiers appeared. The team were all dead pale with sadness as they saw Hans's dying body laid out on the table.

Dia poked his missile launcher through the window and readied a shot so as to keep the team covered. Michael then told Chang to get the medic supplies out while telling the team, "Boys...stay here and give Hans's cover!! I'm going out...to finish what he started...I'll probably be back."

However, Vincent, having just seen Hans get battered, remarked in a horrified tone,
"What? Michael...we can't lose you!! You're our leader!"

"Don't worry lads, you probably won't...stay here! I will be back!!"

Michael grabbed a missile launcher and went out to face the machines but before he could do anything...the machines were suddenly shredded apart by missiles that kept splitting into smaller missiles until they hit their target. Curious, Michael had looked up to see several large flying fortresses flying above the battlefield. They were arrayed in disciplined formations.

The garrison of Edinburgh cheered as they saw the flying fortresses clearing through the machine army. Help had finally arrived at the battlefield as a whole fleet of dropships touched down on the battlefield, deploying their divisions of troops and vehicles. The presence of the reinforcements immediately turned the tide for the Terran forces. Seeing the arrival of the reinforcements, Michael couldn't help but smile because their efforts had resulted in paving the way for a decisive victory in Edinburgh. However, that satisfaction was melted by a sudden jolt of dread which led him to run back over to the house. Upon entering the house, Michael asked, "Boys...what has happened?"

The team all looked up at Michael. Hans's lifeless body lay on the table. It was possible to see bullet holes in the armour and in the flesh of the body.

The team kept their emotions disciplined but Vincent was biting his lip to stop himself from sobbing; as a result, his lips were beginning to bleed. Alexi slowly removed his helmet and made the sign of the cross.

Looking up at Michael, Dermot said to him, "It's too late sir; the bullets had gone too deep ...we couldn't save him!"

This response caused Michael to stare with horror. Slowly, he blessed himself and unstrapped his helmet as he approached the dead body of Hans. There was no humour or joy, because even though they had beaten the enemy, Hans, who had been part of their squad for a long time, was dead. Michael felt the pain as much as Vincent and the others did and when he approached Hans's body, he stroked Hans's face, saying, "Come on, even if he is dead, we bring this boy home."

"Aye...on your orders sir." Vincent responded solemnly.

The Legionnaires won the battle that day. Edinburgh was safe, but Vincent was too grief-stricken to notice. They hauled Hans's deceased body back up the ramp of their dropship. When he saw them entering the dropship, Alonzo asked, "What happened? Were you successful?"

As they lay Hans's deceased body down in the hanger, Alonzo then took off his helmet and made the sign of the cross. The looks of the team were enough to make him realise the gravity of the situation for the team and their pain. He asked no more and went back to the cockpit. With a heavy heart, he flew them back to the *Tungsten*. As the dropship made its rattling journey back to the *Tungsten*, Alonzo sorrowfully played the song 'Angel Flight' on the radio as he kept his gloved hands on the controls.

CHAPTER 3: COST OF WAR

Later on, Jethro watched from the control tower as the dropships touched down onto the decks of the *Tungsten*. Many Legionnaires and Home Guardsmen that had been fighting at Edinburgh were coming off on crutches while others were being carried down the ramps on stretchers. There were also many body bags, which were then transferred onto a truck that would transport them to the freezer to keep them preserved. Finally, the smaller dropship of Team Alpha dropped off the squad. Vincent and Dermot carried off the dead Hans on a stretcher. The sight of this stung Jethro's heart. Rufus came over and looked at the sight below. He seemed emotionless looking at the returning Legionnaires from Edinburgh.

"The cost of war indeed, it comes with the cost of youth, the cost of men," Rufus said to Jethro.

"How have we endured for so long and maintained our dignity? It only took four years of bloodshed to shake and disorient the British empire. We've been fighting this war for as long as Terra has existed."

"Indeed! Old England got too self-confident and self-assured in its own strength! We never made that mistake. No matter, I will inform London and tell them that the city of Edinburgh is safe for resettling its population and that the invasion from the North Sea has been thwarted! A city must be repopulated once it is reclaimed!"

Jethro then asked Rufus, "But sir! The invasion came from a base in the North Sea! The same one that launched the attack on New York in 2345! We cannot just let it exist!"

Rufus responded in a calm and calculated tone. "Colonel, the Terran Arctician fleet operating from the Arctic circle has already engaged with it! The base was destroyed by the Arctician fleet during the battle of Edinburgh. Now if you'll excuse me, I am going to inform London of the news." Before walking off, Rufus added,

"Colonel! When asking about the purpose of fighting, think of the common people and those you know. It makes war slightly more bearable! They fight and die for the survival of the human race."

With that, Rufus left the Control Tower, leaving Jethro standing there. An officer approached Jethro and asked him, "Orders, sir?"

"Set course for the North Pole!"

"Yes, sir!"

* * *

Many nights later in the Arctic Circle, where the Northern lights appeared, a large group of flying fortresses were circling a frozen mountain. On the mountain was a group of Legionnaires. They were in their armour and their uniforms, but they clasped their helmets and caps under their shoulders. They felt the cold icy breeze of the North Pole as many of them built pyres. Upon these pyres they placed dead Legionnaires while a troop of priests marched in a disciplined array. They chanted as they blessed the pyres. The lead priest had a very long beard that stirred in the wind as he grasped a towering golden cross while the other clerics marching behind him were sprinkling the air with incense. The different regiments of Legionnaires from around the world stood to attention. Michael, who had placed Hans's corpse on the pyre, stroked Hans's face while saying in Latin, "Find peace...brother."

He got off the pyre, clasped a burning torch and lit the pyre. The next thing, one by one...many pyres were lit. The smoke and sparks went soaring up into the Northern sky and the fires could be seen for miles. As this happened, Vincent led a regiment of Legionnaires in a haka; as if saluting their fallen brothers who perished in battle in order to keep humanity preserved. It was through this dance that the men channelled their rage and their grief, the energy and emotion that flowed through their bodies. After the haka was done, a volley of riflemen then readied their rifles under the orders of an officer. They fired shots into the air in honour of the men.

As they looked at the sparks of the pyre going up into the air, Dermot asked Michael, "Do you think Jethro's going to find us a new recruit?"

"A new meat ...for our team ...add a high school graduate to our team of professionals! That would be just like him!"

"Commander Faulkner? Sir, I know the pain you have...it grips me deep as well...but not even Legionnaires are immortal...what if another one of us gets killed or worse disbanded ...if we don't get more recruits, our team will die out!"

"Maybe...but we're not ready for it! Not emotionally anyway."

"But sir?"

"Enough! Dermot, I said we are not ready for recruits!"

Michael stormed off as if to be by himself, leaving Dermot to just stare after him numbly. Chang came up from behind.

'What just happened?' He asked Dermot.

'Michael's not ready for new recruits...at least emotionally. But by God, we absolutely need them, we're dying Chang."

"Look on the bright side, if our deaths hurt him, it shows that we're more than just meat to him," Chang remarked, while patting Dermot on the shoulder.

Meanwhile, Rufus was waiting in the main control tower of the *Tungsten*. He seemed unemotional and stoic on the surface as he observed the scene from the control tower. He had seen this ritual again and again; it was a normal sight for him. Despite his unemotional exterior, he was no toxic monster and his heart grieved for the loss of his troops. That being said, he didn't allow his grief to ever get in the way of his coordination of the war effort. He was fighting a war to preserve the human race, against a foe that would accept no peace or diplomatic agreements to cease firing. As Rufus observed the pyres, Jethro approached him from behind.

"Commander Thorne...the new reserves will be arriving, ready to fill up the ranks of our regiments at the front!" Jethro said

"Good, we badly need the support. More offensives are to commence...we cannot let war weariness slow us down...though it drags me deep...we must reclaim as much territory as possible...

is that understood Colonel Jethro?"

"Yes, sir."

Rufus Thorne continued to look at the sparks as they soared up towards the Northern Lights. The souls of the fallen Legionnaires were gone to an afterlife. For Terra, the afterlife was not a place of fighting but a place of peace.

A land where there would be no more wars or suffering or machines. This was the afterlife that all Terrans believed in. Rufus Thorne however had little time to be concerned about the lives of individual Legionnaires. He had a globalised war to handle. He had a heart but when he lost his first unit, he was so grieved by it that he mismanaged his first battle. As a result, he hardened his heart over what had happened and vowed to focus his mind on pure, cold rational thought. After all, it was the way the machines worked; they were programmed to wage war and they had no compassion, just cold logic.

CHAPTER 4: NEW MEATS & NEW OFFENSIVES

Many days had passed since the battle of Edinburgh. The *Tungsten* was currently positioned above the North Sea, ready to deploy troops into Eastern Europe. Currently, the Legion had received new orders from London. The Terran government at Westminster was planning to launch an offensive into the heart of Eurasia, straight through the Ural Mountains so as to reach the machine's industrial complex. The aim was to cripple the robotic war effort and hopefully bring an end to the war. The Terran state was amassing its best flying fortresses for the mission. This fleet was led by the main trio of flying fortresses: The *Tungsten* from which Alpha Squad operated; the *Valiant*, one of the earliest of the flying fortresses built by Terra, and the largest of all the flying fortresses, the *Kirov*.

High above the North Sea, a dropship soared towards the clouds. Zach sat alongside a long line of recruits as he felt the vibration rattling through the hull of the dropship. He had passed his training modules, had undergone the enhancement of having his body modified to be more enduring and more resistant to the elements; just like the other boys that had the bad luck to end up in the Legion. And just like the other boys, he was nervous as hell for the fight ahead. The dropship flew towards the flying fortress *Tungsten,* and the sergeant shouted,

"Come on, up you get lads, we're heading for the *Tungsten,* and from there, you will be located to your designated regiments; blending in will be tough, first they'll hate you but if you earn their respect, they'll grow to love you…so stay focused and stay strong!"

The new meats got up into line. They all wore dark green uniforms and peakless caps. They had backpacks slung over their shoulders. Every one of them, regardless of race, were all short haired and clean shaven.

The sergeant sported the same dark green uniform, but unlike the recruits he had a visored peaked cap. This uniform and peaked cap was the standard uniform of all Terran officers.

When the dropship touched down on the flying fortress, the ramp was lowered. The sergeant yelled, "Go, go, go get out of here. Keep moving. Colonel Jethro expects to see you at the briefing hall."

The rush of freezing cold air brushed around the new meats as they came running out onto the decks towards the control tower of the vessel. Two legionnaires passed them by. One of them said to the other in a humorous tone, "Well, Kowalski ... look at all these fresh puppies. Charming don't you think?"

"Yeah, I bet we won't see them for much longer!"

* * *

At the briefing hall, the recruits had gathered and listened as Jethro addressed them.

"Boys, you are not in civilization anymore!! You are at the front, the very front between man and machine. Only a few more hours, and you'll be moved to separate regiments; after that, you will be taking orders from the commander of your unit! You bear a great burden, boys, we are going on the offensive, reclaiming territory for the human race. How many of you will survive? I really can't answer that for you. There will be many faces that I won't be seeing after this day!"

Zach listened nervously. Only a few more minutes and he would be joining a new group of strangers, but he was braced for it, no matter what happened. So, he waited patiently as the lecture went on.

After all, Zach thought, once you were in the Legion, there was no going back for you. Still the alternative he had was death via execution, so he did have some chance at being alive. If he died, he'd go down in history as someone defending his country rather than someone who murdered another. For most Terrans, that demise was slightly more bearable. Very few ever wanted to go to the grave as a criminal.

* * *

That evening, Michael smoked a cigar as he peered over the decks of the flying fortress. So-called 'new meats' were now filling up spare ranks in the northern detachments. Michael felt that he already had enough with five squad troopers to deal with. At least those men were self-sufficient and well capable of handling themselves without him. The last thing that Michael felt he needed was a new recruit who would potentially be dependent on him in the heat of the battle.

It was at that moment that he heard a young American-sounding voice ask, "Captain Faulkner? Sir?"

Michael turned around to face a young white, dark haired and blue-eyed young man. Both curious and angry, Michael said "what?" to the recruit.

"Sir, I'm private Zach Harker! Eh is this the residence of Alpha Squad, also known as Team Orca?"

"What of it?"

"Well, I was sent to replace deceased Legionnaire Hans...I..."

"No, you're not..."

"I'm following orders, sir...I"

"Stay here! I'm going to talk to Jethro!"

Seeing Jethro behind Zach on the decks, Michael stormed past Zach and towards Jethro. Facing Jethro in the eyes, he snapped,

"Colonel, this boy will drop like a fly...please take him off the list and pair him with his own age group."

"Oh no, these boys are reserves...I'm not the one who makes the choices. Commander Thorne is."

"But my men, they will...they will treat him with the most utter contempt, he will mean nothing to them, sir!"

"Michael, I need you to trust me, never forget that you lot were just new meat at one point...never forget that!"

"Colonel!! I may not trust this boy...but I will never let you down sir!"

Michael's coal black eyes turned to face Zach.

"So, you are taking me, sir?" Zach asked.

"Well, what can I say?... I have no choice. Follow me!"

Michael led Zach to a hatch that he opened up and let Zach crawl in. As he crawled in, Zach could hear laughter in the sleeping quarters where the rest of the team were waiting. Zach entered the sleeping quarters to see three of them playing cricket. A cricket ball missed the bat and Zach caught it in his hand. They all looked at him with either curiosity or suspicion. Seeing the sight of all these muscular and seemingly hostile men, Zach muttered

"Hey g.... oh shit!"

A deep voice sounded across the sleeping quarters saying sarcastically

"'Oh, shit'! Is that how a new meat addresses his comrades?"

"Eh Sorry, I'm Zach...I didn't mean to..."

The voice suddenly calmed down and said in a comforting and amused tone, "Hey, it's okay, relax, man, I'm guessing you are new here kid, are you? Everybody gets scared on their first day here."

"Yes, I mean yes sir. I am the new kid...yeah."

Zach composed himself as he observed the sleeping quarters. It was then the bat holder asked in his Scottish sounding tone, "Aye...you lost new meat?"

"Eh, well no, I'm assigned here to be part of your squad. Colonel Jethro's orders."

Another trooper, Vincent, got up from his bed, but the Scotsman simply said, "Eh okay, so little Zach, I'm Dermot, the sniper of the team, and the one who threw the ball that you caught is Dia. Don't worry, he's a good lad to be around. Come on laddie, settle down and make yourself at home."

"Thanks Dermot, I hope I'm not going to be too much of a problem to you."

However, as Zach walked further into the room, Vincent asked angrily, "Hey, you? You a new meat? What the fuck are you doing here?"

"I'm Zach, I'm here because I've been ordered to join your squadron!"

"Oh, are you new meat? You look skimpy and pathetic, just

as we expected from your type. You're the last thing we need on our team!"

Zach turned from being afraid to being frustrated with the hostility, so he snapped back... "Yeah, alright, I haven't even gotten your name yet. Look, if you don't like me being on your team, go talk to Commander Thorne, I'm sure he doesn't have the time for your complaints anyway."

Furious, Vincent clenched his fists. "Alright you, buckle up you spunky brat, this goes for any cocky new meat that thinks he can take Hans's place!"

Vincent readied his fist and he could have destroyed Zach's face at that moment had Dermot not pushed Vincent back. Angry himself, Dermot snapped at Vincent. "Hey, mind your own fucking business Vincent, Zach is new to the team, so what? We were all new once!"

"Damn you Dermot...we didn't slow each other down...he will..."
"Who says he will..."

Everybody looked anxiously as Vincent got up and glared Dermot in the eyes.

"Are you challenging me Dermot? After all this time, for a little mutt who is standing in the shoes of my best and closest buddy, Hans. How dare you think we can just befoul his legacy! And listen, he spoke arrogantly to me! He's not even a man!! Let alone a Legionnaire!" Vincent said in his deep New Zealander accent.

"Jesus Christ, Vincent, chill the fuck down, Hans didn't save you in Berlin so that you could act like a prick! You and Hans did your best to keep as many new meats alive as possible!"

Furious, Vincent swished his fist, but Dermot stepped aside, causing him to slam his fist into Alexi's bunk. Alexi woke up disoriented. Zach was bewildered at what had developed into a boxing fight between Dermot and Vincent, while Chang and Dia looked bemused and surprised at the whole thing.

"What just happened? That escalated very quickly." Chang said.

"Vincent doesn't like our recruit! Come on let's stop this

before Michael comes…"

But before Dia and Chang could do anything to stop the fight, the door opened wide and in came Michael. All excitement ended at the sight of his glaring eyes.

Alexi, who had just woken up to the boxing fight said, "Well, welcome back sir, seems that you missed a scrap?"

"I've just come in Alexi and I'm not in the mood to laugh. What's the row about?"

"Ah, poor Vincent, he lost his temper. He doesn't seem too welcoming to our newcomer!" Dermot responded in a pitiful voice

"Well, that is the selection process, not my choice. Zach is on the team, and I can't change that! So, you better get on with him."

Michael then went up to face Vincent in the eyes, forcibly lowering Vincent's fist. Panicking and angry, Vincent said, "What the…What the f…"

"I don't want to warn you again. Regardless of whether he's a little twerp or not, if I catch you socking him I'll administer the same penalty as I do if I caught you socking up anyone else that is flesh and blood! I'll break your arm!"

"Over him? Sir?"

"I really would. So, don't push me."

Michael let go of Vincent, leaving him to retreat to his bunk. Zach shivered as Michael said in a menacing, deep voice; "Zach, if I find that you are the aggressor the same penalty goes for you!"

"Don't worry, sir! I don't intend on provoking you anytime soon, sir!"

"Good boy, I still have to get myself to like you but you're under my charge so God helps anyone who tries to sock you. Your bunk is above that of Alexi!"

Zach took a deep breath as he climbed up onto his bunk with his gear bag.

"Enjoying it already?" Alexi asked.

"Not much to enjoy here, is there? How do you guys stick with one another? You act like assholes to each other!"

"This is not a normal situation. You see Zach, we've been invincible until Hans's death. Vincent is just scared that a new meat might screw up our reputation as the glamorous elite. As for Michael, he needs to be tough; How else is he in charge? You don't lead men by being the sugar plum fairy! Sweet dreams! You'll understand when you've been in the army for most of your life."

"Yeah, thanks for the advice, man."

Vincent retreated into his bunk, but an obvious sense of anger and embarrassment developed in his mind as he looked up at Zach's bunk. The brute truth was that he hadn't had time to get over Hans's death. It was then that Dia asked him in a whispering tone, "Vincent, you know that boy is not to blame for what happened to Hans, nor is he to blame for the order to bring him in here, don't you?"

"Dia, it's not simply about Hans. I mean look at the twerp. We've been through hell and back for as long as I can remember, but him, I wonder what experience he has? He could screw us up in a second! Thorne in his ivory tower should put more thought into such decisions."

"I know, I fear that too, but by God, we have to give the boy a chance. Maybe you'll be absolutely right, or maybe you could be wrong. A man is only as tough as you allow him to be. Let's not forget, we were once like him."

"But we were all at the same level, we've moved past that. He hasn't…"

Dia and Vincent went quickly mute as Michael approached. He looked at them briefly before heading off.

CHAPTER 5: ZACH'S NIGHTMARE

Zach took in another deep breath, pondering on the names and physical characteristics of his new team. Dermot was the youngest of them. Like the others, he was muscular. He was clean shaven, had green eyes and short light brown hair. Dia had dark nut-brown skin and was bald. Alexi had tattoos of runes and dragons all over him, a moustache and a very closely cropped yet spikey army haircut. Chang had short black hair and a mostly clean-shaven look and Vincent had tanned skin, had short coal black hair and his muscular body had Māori tattoos. Michael had a Byronic appearance with tanned skin, very short, curly, coal black hair and coal black eyes.

Zach closed his eyes and settled down to sleep. But sleep didn't come easily that night as he started to dream of the day when his father died. That was the day of the siege of New York in 2345 when he was seven; he was blonde back then. Zach could never forget that day back in New York city.

* * *

One moment they were in the museum, having just had a photograph taken of them and then the next thing, the air raid sirens went off leaving himself, his family and practically everyone in New York rushing to the shelters. Zach could barely think to himself as he clung onto his father's hand. He clutched onto his stuffed rabbit. He could hear the thunder of the machine battleship's enormous guns firing off from the Atlantic. However, all Zach could do was keep running and stay with his family till they reached the shelter. All of a sudden, Zach dropped his stuffed toy in the panic. At that time, it was something he just couldn't lose so Zach literally tried to rush back despite his father desperately calling him by name. But Zach felt the need to go back, even though most civilians had rushed onwards towards a shelter. However, not far from where he was, an artillery shell sliced through a skyscraper causing it to collapse and come tumbling down, crashing into the ground. A ton of debris could have fallen on Zach had his father not grabbed onto the little boy and rolled him out of the way. Zach could barely hear anything, but he did hear the screams of people that, like him, were caught in the middle of the explosions caused by the battleships bombarding New York. Above a flying fortress and several dropships equipped with torpedoes rushed out towards the coastline in hope of destroying the battleships.

Zach was then grasped in his father's arms and looked into his icy eyes with a mix of anger and emotion.

"Zach, what do you think you're doing? You want to get yourself killed? Over a stuffed animal?"

"But Dad, he's my only one...I?"

"Zach, we can always get another rabbit, but we can't just go into the shop and buy another Zach, alright? Damn you, you're too good to die!"

Then the noise of a siren heralded what looked to be an armoured van with a searchlight, that came hurtling towards them. Zach's father lifted him up as the vehicle approached. There was the sound of babbling in a radioed American voice before the vehicle came to a halt. Out of the vehicle came two men in greenish-yellow chemical protection suits. One of them yelled out asking:

"Hey, sir? Where's your designated air raid shelter?"

"Sir!! You're under arrest for not following the codes of evacuation and ignoring the orders of the air raid wardens!" The other one yelled.

As they said this, they came closer to Niall with the intention of detaining him.

"Please keep your palms together, you'll be held in detention until..."

Panicked and scared by what was happening, Niall just yelled out to the men saying, "Hey wait, WAIT, WAIT, WAIT! What are you doing? I had to retrieve my son! My name is Niall Harker, and my designated shelter is Eco, my wife and younger son are waiting there, just let me get there, drop off Zach and..."

The two men looked at each other.

"Shelter Eco has been closed because it has been filling up quickly,

at this rate, it may be reaching its total capacity." One of them said.

"Come on, we know how big Terran shelters are. They are giant vaults, surely, we still have enough room for these two guys; don't we?"

Before the other man could respond to his comrade's response, they heard the ship's big guns again and saw several shells come flying over their location. Fortunately for now, they seemed to be missing them.

However, one of the shells that hit down the street was a canister of some sort. It bounced off the ground at least three times before suddenly cracking. Upon hitting the ground, it started to spew a dark greenish yellow mist...a salvo of chlorine gas. It swirled up into a cloud, only to rush through the streets as if it was some sort of wild beast and it was coming right to where Niall and the others were.

"Right, come on! We need to go!" One of the men said to his comrade.

"But wait, you can't just leave us!! Zach's got a life ahead of him!"

"We have no time; our vehicle only has enough room for one more person!!"

Desperate to make sure he didn't come out for nothing, Niall yelled to the men as he pushed Zach forward.

"Then take my son!!"

"What? But Dad...I"

"Zach, I know what you're thinking, but these guys know what they're doing, you've got a longer life ahead of you, Zach. Go on, you can trust these gentlemen."

"But what will I say to Mom?"

"Come on, kid, that's it, they'll take you to your momma alright?"

Zach nodded reluctantly, but he suddenly stopped feeling his father's warm gloves and soon felt the rather cold tight grip of one of the wardens as he was held onto by one of them. As a warden dragged Zach away, he reached out for Niall.

"Dad, we'll meet again, won't we? Dad?"

Niall was speechless as he and Zach looked each other in the eyes. But the warden just rushed towards the truck as his colleague yelled, "Bill, come on, we need to get out of here!!"

"Alright, Ralph, I'm coming. Come on, sonny, no time for a cute goodbye!"

Niall tried to maintain his composure as he saw the two wardens dump little Zach into the back of the truck. Zach was speechless with guilt and grief, but he could only look back to see his father. For a while, Niall tried following the truck but then he stopped, gasping for breath. The gas was rushing closer and closer. Niall thrust his hand into his pocket to pull out his gas mask. There was nothing there. Niall went pale. He watched the back of the van receding, tears streaming down his face.

Zach could only look back in fear and sadness as he looked at his father one last time. That was the last time he got to look at Niall before the young, pale skinned, dark haired and blue-eyed figure that was his father disappeared under the green-yellow mist. Zach then slumped back. He was speechless simply because of his guilt. It was all over a mere stuffed rabbit that he rushed out, and, in his eyes, got his father gassed.

* * *

The shelters of Terra were large, underground networks of shopping facilities, sleeping quarters, metro train networks and other services, including hospitals. Zach's mom, Valentine, was waiting near the entrance of the shelter looking for her husband and her son. The wardens arrived with Zach. Valentine, surprised and relieved, briefly embraced Zach but when she noticed that Niall wasn't with him, a feeling of dread crept over her.

"Hey wait, where's Niall?"

"Niall?"

"My husband, Niall Harker, do you know where he is?"

"Sorry lady, we only had room for one more person in our vehicle, and he knew that all too well!!"

Valentine's skin got even paler than it naturally was while her sapphire blue eyes widened.

"What? You..."

"Just get back to your place in the shelter. This bombardment could go on for hours. The shelters will provide everything you need"

"But..."

Valentine slumped back against a wall. Her face was starting to go red as she clung onto both boys. She slowly slid down to the ground, trying very hard to keep back her tears. The thunder of the guns on both sides raged on overhead as the battle continued. Valentine and Niall were in their mid-twenties when this happened. Niall wasn't the classic hero, but he had the heart to stay with her and stick up for her in college, even after he accidentally got her pregnant. Now she had two boys, Zach and Phil, and she had a job in the local bar...but she felt alone. Probably more alone than both the boys felt. Trying to hold her tears back, she looked into the eyes of both of her children, snuggling them both. It would be a long time before the raid on New York would be finally over. The machine battleships eventually retreated back to their base in the North Sea, having inflicted a brutally successful terror attack.

* * *

For the rest of the day, Zach was very much mute since the moment he last saw his father disappear under that thick green mist. He wouldn't eat or even cry, and that evening, after everything was done and the threat was over, he just sat there on the bed staring into space, his eyes open very wide. He wasn't staring at anything in particular. Valentine came into the bedroom after having putting Phil to sleep, and she sat down on the bed beside Zach.

"Zach? Hey Zach?"

Zach turned around to look her in the eyes. The boy's distraught face told her everything she needed to know about how he felt. Leaning down beside him, Valentine tried to ask cheerfully,

"Zach? I've got something for you."

She handed him the stuffed rabbit that he might have died for had his father not got him out of the way. Zach took a brief look at the rabbit, but it brought him no joy because it just reminded him of what led to his father's death. He tossed it aside. Valentine felt as if her heart was melting.

"Zach, please just speak to me honey...come on...I..."

Zach stayed motionless; he seemed to be just staring. Valentine let *out a sigh as she got off the bed and walked towards the door.*

"I'll see you in the morning, Zach."

Her face had a sad expression when she turned around to flick off the lights and leave the room. That was until she flicked the lights off and heard Zach suddenly cry out, "Wait!"

Valentine turned around in surprise to hear Zach suddenly call out for her. She turned on the lights and looked into his heart wrenched eyes.

"Please Mom!! I don't want to lose you as well!"

"Zach, come on, I'm not going to leave you, honey."

Valentine knelt down to clasp Zach tightly in her arms. The boy's face was buried in her nightgown as it became wet with his tears. Valentine tried her best to comfort Zach but even she was on the verge of crying herself because her husband was now dead; probably going to be among the many cremated tomorrow night. However, she managed not to cry.

"Zach, do you want to sleep alongside me for the night?"

He didn't answer, but he clung onto her, strongly implying yes. Valentine took Zach up in her arms, carrying him into her bedroom and laying him onto the bed next to her.

* * *

At that moment he woke up. Scrambling up from under his bedsheets, he realised that was back in his bunk, in the sleeping quarters of the *Tungsten*. As he was sleeping on one of the higher bunk beds, Zach took a long while to make himself comfortable because such bunk beds were not as comfortable as the warm soft beds back home, the type that Zach used to sleep before he ended up in the army. He took a look at the digital clock beside his bed and found that it was twelve midnight. Everyone else around him was asleep, so he dozed off again.

***

Several hours later, he could hear Dermot's voice calling him by name, slowly opening his eyes to the sound of Dermot's voice.

"Zach? Zach?"

Zach sat up rather clumsily, feeling very disoriented due to being woken up.

"Eh, what just happened?" Zach asked.

"Come on get up! Michael would be mad if you were late!"

Hearing the word 'late' caused Zach to spring out of bed like a jack in the box. He then started to suit up into his uniform as quickly as possible. He did not want to be late for his first full routine on a flying fortress. Not keeping up in routine could mean the difference between life and death. Plus, he had seen enough of Michael to not want to be on his bad side.

CHAPTER 6: ADAPTING TO A NEW LIFE

The following day was just Zach getting to know his surroundings, trying on his new armour and drilling in preparation for the rush hour. "Rush Hour" was a nickname given by the troops to the beginning of the great offensive. Zach tried his best to blend in with the squad, but it was one of the most difficult things he ever had to do.

Dermot was the only one he really got on with. Many other legionnaires looked at him oddly; this was the fate of many new recruits. The sergeants had to watch the men like hawks in order to protect the new meats. Jethro kept them hard at it.

* * *

That evening, Zach just felt lonely. He was only eighteen and most of the team were all mature adults. He was little more than a boy surrounded by men. Dermot was lying down on the opposite bunk to Zach while the others were playing poker. Dermot was used to being the youngest of the team before Zach came on, so he knew all too well what it was like to be alone due to being younger than the rest of the team.

"You're not going to join in?" Dermot asked Zach in a concerned tone.

"I feel out of place here...why does Vincent hate me so much? Was it because I said 'shit' at the start? Look, I didn't choose to be in this squad. Commander Thorne did."

"Zach...it's much deeper than that, we lost Hans, and Hans was Vincent's best buddy throughout his time in the Legion...the death weighs heavy on him. Don't worry about it, it's not your fault. Wait till we end up in a war zone, he'll be nothing but glad to have you!"

Zach tried to smile as best he could as Dermot patted him on the back. The chatter continued until the hatch in the door began to turn, opening the door.

Michael entered the room, causing the team to stand up.

"Boys, we've got news. The offensive is going to take place tomorrow! We will be piercing into the frontlines of the machines so that we can do as much damage to their industrial sector beyond the Urals as possible. If it makes you more comfortable, we'll have the benefit of aerial and heavy armoured support. They'll try to help you as best they can, but they can only do so much. When it comes to fighting it will be up to you. You, Zach especially, you want to be considered a Legionnaire, you want to be honoured by Terra, tomorrow is your chance!"

"What do we do tonight, sir?" Alexi asked Michael.

Michael thought for a moment, but then he said rather staunchly,

"Well, there is all too much of a chance that one of us could die tomorrow!! So, for tonight, while all of us are still breathing...we drink!!"

* * *

That night, Zach felt both fear and excitement as he entered the bar with the rest of his team. This was his first night as a legionnaire and they were out for a drink before their mission commenced. The moment Zach entered the bar he was surrounded by both rookies like himself and hardened Legionnaires. Everybody had the same kind of uniform, regardless of skin, class, origin or religion, he was a Legionnaire and a Terran. And they were all equally at the mercy of the same cruel rules.

As they wandered through the bar and passed by all the different groups of troops, Dermot said to Zach, "Well, laddie, since this is your first time in the bar, I feel that it is your duty to inform you about the different units that come to this bar; see those guys with closely cropped heads, they're the tankers and they operate the tanks. They go for a very close crop so that their helmets can fit onto their heads; their helmets look like some sort of virtual reality device. They stick to themselves, they can be very vulgar, and they love their machines as if they were their lovers; so, if you don't want to be boxed, don't insult their tanks."

He then pointed to the bar counter at another large group.

"See those guys with the smart, dark green uniforms, peaked caps and tidy haircuts? They are the aeronauts and they man the aviation, especially behemoths like the flying fortresses. They try to maintain their manners; they're well educated but they like to brawl with tankers. They look very handsome and pretty but they ain't softies, keeping a flying fortress airborne is a life and death struggle in of itself! Their skin and bones were modified to be tougher so as to resist the sudden thrusts of speed when flying a jet!"

"Do we brawl with either group?" Zach asked.

"Ah, it's best not to do that; it causes unnecessary rivalry problems, petty rivalries can damage a force that uses combined arms like us! It's the last thing that we need!"

"Yeah, thanks for the advice."

Legionnaires would often drink, play games and settle their disputes on the ring.

Popular ballads like "General Taylor" and "Jakey's Gin" could be heard from the radios. Zach felt nervous as everybody, especially the elites, glared at him. The team eventually reached the bar counter where the barkeep waited. Even he looked menacing. He was muscular and had a tanned, well-built body. He was bald and clean shaven. He turned around when he saw the team, staring at Zach.

"So, Mic? Any special offers for your hot newcomer?" He asked in a deep, Southern American voice.

"Just get him some water, the rest of us, same as usual, shots of Heineken and Guinness."

Zach looked around him as the barkeep filled the cups.

"You ever been in a bar before?" Alexi asked.

"Believe it or not, I have, since I was six years old. My mother works in a bar back in New York. She needed to work nightshifts at times to keep our income coming because my Dad got killed in a bombardment, and she had both me and my younger brother to stick out for."

"What age is she?"

"About thirty-seven; she still lives with my younger brother today."

"Thirty-seven, and you are already eighteen? Okay, she started young. Zach, is she nice?"

"She was relatively gorgeous, I guess. I mean she and my Dad did fall for each other when they were both eighteen. There were times where it probably seemed like she hated me, but overall, she loves us to bits."

"So then, let me ask you, if she loved you so much then why did you leave her to join a bunch of assholes like us?"

"I had no choice, my brother and I got jumped by a gang, and the leader was about to carve a Glaswegian grin on our faces until I got my switch knife and stabbed the guy and in doing so, I killed him. My brother was safe, but I got arrested for murder. Thus, it was either the Legion or the electric chair for me. Besides, they gave a healthy compensation to the families of the boys who undergo the process of being genetically modified! Why are you so interested in my backstory, Alexi?"

"I don't know, maybe because you sleep in the bunk above me, or maybe because I want to know how an adolescent New Yorker ended up in our squad. Since we're stuck with you, I might as well get to know you."

"Thank you for making the effort."

Zach allowed himself to smile this time round. Slowly but surely, he was starting to feel more comfortable in his surroundings. It was best that he made himself comfortable, after all, it was basically his new home. The barkeep handed out the beers on a tray and the group moved over to a table. The squad then raised their drinks as Michael said, "A toast! A toast to Hans; I hope the afterlife is more peaceful for him ...and a toast to the endurance of our squad!"

"Cheers!!"

Zach nervously clinked his glass with the others.

***

Later that night, Zach thought quietly to himself. He missed his family, but he had no choice. He had murdered the bully and there was no favourable witness on his side. Since his mother was working at the bar during that time, she wasn't there to witness, meaning that she was powerless to protect him, and his little brother was too small to stand in court. He hoped that his family was better off with the pension they got for allowing him to go. He was too afraid to talk to others about it.

It took a long time for Zach to get to sleep that night. He didn't know how but he knew that he would not emerge the same as he was when he entered the Terran military. If he died, that would be his life story cut violently short by bullets and if he survived, he would be a different man. He even wondered if his father would recognise him now as he was. The fleet of flying fortresses continued their journey through the night sky. Their use of nuclear fusion cores ensured that they were capable of going to a location nonstop for years. Technology like this played an important role in keeping Terra in the fight.

CHAPTER 7: THE ATTACK ON SAINT PETERSBURG

The lights flashed red, signifying that the *Tungsten* was getting close to St Petersburg and urging the legionnaires out of their sleeping quarters. As they suited up, Zach asked Dermot, Alexi and Chang, "Guys, before the battle do we get a chance to contact our parents or our siblings?"

Chang responded rather solemnly to Zach's question by saying

"We do, but most of us don't have a family."

"What? No family?"

"We lost ours in the war. But we may have no family, but we have each other!"

"Wait, you lot are family? Well, from what I saw, you have a great way of showing it." Zach replied,

The three looked at each other, but it was time for the regiments to move on to the briefing room.

In the briefing room the men sat in ranks. Rufus Thorne presented to them the key mission objectives on a map.

"Gentlemen, the offensive is going to commence today. However, our reports have discovered a machine offensive heading for the city of Saint Petersburg. As a result, your mission is to head for Saint Petersburg and defend it from the machines. While the battle is in motion you will maintain control of the key airports and fortresses. Now, the tricky part is that a machine force is heading in hot, you will have to take the entrenchments as well in order to hold the line. We are ready to give as much support as possible but if the battle goes ill, you will evacuate the civilian population to the dropships which will take them to refugee camps in either Germany or Norway. Once there we will regroup to continue the offensive! Is that clear?"

"Yes, sir!" The Legionnaires responded.

"Good!! May God be with you all!"

Once the briefing was complete, the troops left the room to

get ready for the attack.

Later on, Legionnaires were lining up to contact their families. As Zach joined the queue, the rest of the squad waited for him.

"You have to admit, Captain, you'd want your family to know you love them if you were going out to war. Wouldn't you?" Dia said to Michael.

"I know, but I don't have a family…except for you boys."

Zach was nervous as he dialled in his mother's phone number.

In New York, Valentine's phone buzzed in her pocket while she was serving some customers. She wasn't supposed to answer her phone while serving but the barkeep, James said, "Hey Valentine, I think your phone just went off there…maybe you should answer it."

"I'll be back in a few minutes," Valentine said to a customer, after a pause.

She slipped away to a private area to answer the call. Her heart skipped a beat when she heard Zach's voice.

"Hey, Mom …it's me, Zach. You probably haven't heard from me for a while!"

"Zach? Oh, thank God you're still alright…have you something to tell me?"

"Look, Mom, are you still working in that bar?"

"Well, I've been doing it so long I'm used to it now, so my life hasn't changed that much."

"Mom it might change in a big way. The battle is on, so this is probably the last time you'll hear from me for a while. I'm with a bunch of assholes, but I've gone too far to drop out…so just tell Phil that I love him."

"I'll try, but Zach you're not a semi-immortal superhero so don't risk your life, because even if you're the noob of your team I still love you to bits!"

"Thanks, Mom, don't be scared, I won't stay a little boy forever. Goodbye."

Valentine slipped her phone back into her pocket as James came in.

"How's your boy keeping?"

Valentine turned around and pulled herself together.

"He's doing well, thanks."

James smiled.

"Good, his old man would be proud!"

"How would you know, James? Niall might have wanted his son to be a man but not a killing machine!"

James sighed.

"Valentine, I've known Niall since he was a boy. Legionnaires aren't conscienceless killing machines; Zach is still himself. Come on, we need to get back to work. Customers are getting impatient."

Valentine followed James back out to the bar.

* * *

Back at the flying fortress *Tungsten*, Zach put down the phone before re-joining his squad.

"So, you are missing your mummy yet?" Vincent said, mockingly.

"Is that something to be ashamed of? I'm not!"

"You...f..."

Frustrated with the arguing, Michael snapped.

"Boys! That's enough! We are Legionnaires, not politicians! Now come on! We don't have much time!"

The troops made their way to the armoury, which was where the Legionnaires assembled their gear and equipment before heading out onto the landing platforms and into the dropships.

As Zach's team got into the dropship, the pilot, Alonzo then said.

"Hey welcome aboard, Team Orca!"

"And you too, Alonzo! You're all checked up right?"

"Don't worry boys, the check is completed, we're ready to go! Brace yourselves!"

Some of the larger dropships were being packed with vehicles ranging from APCs to lightly armoured but quick twin turreted tanks and even massive, armoured vehicles rolling on six huge wheels that had both big guns and missile launchers on their backs. Once everything was packed, the dropships took off towards St Petersburg. Feeling hot and sweaty, Zach clung tight to his assault rifle during the rocky journey as the dropship flew through the heavy winds and towards the objective. It was hard to relax during the bumpy, rattling journey of the dropship and the motion caused him to feel sick. He looked into the eyes of his comrades around him. Shivers ran through his spine because while he trained for warfare like this, this was his first time in action.

* * *

Meanwhile down in St Petersburg, the gleaming colourful domes of the Church of the Saviour on Spilled Blood still stood tall and strong. Along with other orthodox churches it stood out among the long-complicated monorail and high-speed train networks that linked the city with other key cities throughout Europe. The city itself was linked together by immense motorways on which flocks of cars and buses running on hydrogen fuel cells drove across. Aircraft which ran on hover jets flew across the sky above the city. Decorating the streets were statues that looked as if they were keeping their eyes on the populace below. Regiments of the Home Guard kept a watchful eye on the city. Though they were merely ordinary humans, they were ready to make their stand against the machines and defend their homeland. Their entrenchments and their network of defence turrets would be ready should a machine attack occur. At that moment, civilians were going about their usual business.

Many of the civilians in St Petersburg were dressed in winter outfits such as long, fur coats, boots, gloves and furry hats. Many others had bonnets and visored flat caps made out of wool to keep them warm in the icy freezing environment around them. Very few of them were aware that their city was a target which the machines were currently heading for.

But in a radar post on the outskirts of the city, two air raid wardens noticed something. Seeing large red blimps heading towards the city, one warden said to his co-worker, "Igor! Look over here...I've got something on the radar!"

Igor came to look over his shoulder.

"Have you Andrei? Let's see...what do we have here?"

Seeing the blips, Igor suddenly said, "Shit...Machine bombers coming hot! Andrei come on! We need to sound the alarm!"

The air raid sirens let out a piercing wail as wardens rushed out to warn everyone and get them into the shelters. There was mass panic. Despite the warden's best efforts to keep the crowd under control, the rush to the shelters became a disorganised mess, leading many people to be trampled and others to be separated from each other. Vehicles came crashing to a halt as people burst out of them to rush to the shelters. Within moments, practically every single form of public transport, be they buses, trains, monorails or subterranean trains all came screeching to a halt. Meanwhile troops of Home Guardsmen travelled in convoys of armoured vehicles up to reinforce the entrenchments around the city, beeping their horns to warn people to get out of the way.

Seeing the chaos that was developing all around, a young man picked up his son saying

"Dimitri! It's okay, I've got you! Stay with me, honey."

Turning to a young woman with long blonde hair beside him, the man, Nicholas, said to her "Anya, hold onto my hand, we need to get to the underground!"

The three did their best to stay together in the panic and density of the fleeing mob of civilians. The wardens and police did their best to keep order and make sure that the process was as calm as possible. The garrison of the city activated every air defence system possible. Both manned and remote-controlled defences were activated in preparation so as to fight back against oncoming air assaults.

Already a fleet of machine bombers was coming in towards Saint Petersburg. The machine bombers were essentially massive, self-propelled eight-engine aircraft. When their bombing doors opened, hails of bombs fell like raindrops, causing serious amounts of damage. The Home Guard garrison desperately tried to shoot them down, only to have their SAM installations destroyed. Flames spread violently through the buildings as they started to catch fire.

Squadrons of fire engines rushed out to fight the fires and control the damage that was now overwhelming their city. For all their bravery however, the water that emitted out of the firefighters' hoses did very little to quench the raging fires. Nevertheless, the Home Guard scrambled what remaining defences they had and continued to fire at the bombers in an attempt to shoot them down.

Fortunately, friendly fighters showed up and started to shoot down the bombers. Then the bombers launched their drones to fight back against the encroaching interceptors. The flying fortresses were entering the airspace to take part in the battle. The machines responded by sending in their own frigates. These were equally as capable and as well-equipped as the flying fortresses. They were smaller and easier to take down, but they came in larger squadrons than their Terran counterparts.

The battle in the airspace above St Petersburg soon accelerated. An aerial battle in which aircraft from either side of the battle could come crashing down was enough to make the streets unsafe for civilians.

When that happened, the aircraft crashed into a building, ripping through the fabric of the construction, spilling debris all over the place. If the aircraft didn't hit into a building it went straight into a street and it exploded, emitting flame and destroying everything around it.

It was amidst the chaos of this air battle that the dropships of the Legion were touching down to aid their mortal allies, the Home Guard. Already in the heat of a living nightmare, the soldiers waited in their trenches. They could already see large shapes in the distance. These shapes were the machine armoured divisions, so they readied their defences to brace for the oncoming attack. Giant armoured tank-like vehicles arrived on the outskirts of the city and deployed huge numbers of robotic soldiers who then attacked the entrenchments *en masse*.

"Lord God, there are so many of them," one of the men remarked, in pure terror.

Since several of these Guardsmen were new recruits, their

hearts pounded very quickly, and their bodies shivered as they saw the oncoming enemy. They raised their rifles in anticipation and some even just fired rounds of bullets out of panic. Older, more experienced men braced for the intense bombardment that preceded the attack. Though their trenches were strong and deep enough to resist the bombardment, it was very loud, leaving many with sore ears. Smoke quickly covered the battlefield and enveloped the trenches. What then followed was the clanking noise of countless numbers of machine soldiers that spilled out of the vehicles. The vibration of all those numbers caused the area to shake. Their skeletal bodies and blood red eyes made for an intimidating sight for normal humans as they emerged from the smoke. The lead robot then said in a deep and horrible metallic voice: "You have your orders, destroy any organic material. Purge all organics. Execute these orders."

Upon hearing those orders, the machines started to pick up pace, running faster and faster until they all let out an unsettling and artificial roar. As they let out that roar, the machines charged very quickly. They had no need to worry about stamina or food. Only by destroying them outright could you fight and defeat them. They had no fear, yet they had some awareness of how scary they were to humans, so they used everything they had to intimidate humanity as they charged towards the entrenched Home Guard.

Though the garrison of Saint Petersburg put up a hard fight, they started to get overrun by the machines. This wasn't simply a battle; they were in the middle of a massacre as they were torn and ripped apart by the machines. Some machines even bit and dismembered them. They fought back with all they could, emptying their rounds of machine guns and their rockets upon the machines. As he managed to take down another machine, one Guardsman asked his comrade angrily, "Damn it! Where are those Legionnaires when we need them?"

"Up in the air? Their flying fortresses are in the midst of a battle!"

"Fuck! We need them down here now! Our comrades are being ripped to shreds!"

Looming behind the two troopers was a scorpion shaped robot with two machine guns in place of pincers. It had buzz saws on its tail, and it seemed to be eyeing up the two men with its blood red eyes. Horrified, the two men readied their machine guns. At that moment bullets from above ripped the scorpion bot to shreds. Looking up, the men saw the dropship of Alpha Squad sweeping across the battlefield. Many more, larger dropships came flying towards the city, leading the exhausted Guardsmen to cheer as support had finally come. Several of them made the sign of the cross as if to thank God for the fact that the Legion had come to support them.

Alpha Squad's dropship swooped down and strafed the landing area before touching down. As it touched down, the squad fitted on their gas masks and stood up as the lights in the hull flashed red, alerting them to make ready. Then the lights flashed green, the ramp went down, and a burst of freezing cold air invaded the cargo bay as the team rushed out to cover. Zach didn't even know where they were going but he followed his comrades on gut instinct. He knew that if he was going to survive, he had to stay with the group and follow whatever orders Michael had to give them. Once they got into cover, they started to fire at the encroaching machines. Panicked by the battle that was going all around him, Zach just blazed his machine gun anywhere he could see, hitting several machines but not taking any down. He kept blazing his gun until it jammed.

In a panic, he fiddled around with his rifle to get it to shoot again. A canister bounced near him, causing gas to come spewing out in the vicinity. Even though he had his gas mask on and was well protected, the sight of gas left Zach in an infantile panic, a prisoner of the memory of what happened to his father. The machines loomed towards him in the hope of getting close enough to jab him with their bayonets. Seeing the skeletal shapes of the robots with their blood red eyes emerge from the gas did not help soothe the terror that he was starting to feel. Seeing such monsters come so effortlessly through the thick green gas made Zach feel as if he were already dead and had gone to hell. He continued to scramble back across the now battered tarmac as the robots approached him. It was the first time that he had seen such robots up close. Indeed, they looked like they had come straight out of a nightmare as their skeletal bodies had clawed hands and clawed feet. They had racks of ammo attached to their body and a formidable array of grenades attached around their waists. They continued to make a clunking noise as they approached. Their faces looked soullessly down at Zach.

Zach readied his rifle to fire up at the machines in the hope of making one last stand, his hands shaking as he raised his rifle. The rest of the team were taking heavy fire but Dia, seeing Zach in such a helpless state, rushed over to him, grabbing him and dragging him over the gravel to cover. When Zach started to sit up, he then shouted at Zach saying, "Zach! You're not using your gun properly. Spraying bullets everywhere is a quick way to empty your gun!! Just breathe…squeeze…kill…repeat!"

Zach was breathless, both out of exhaustion and terror.

"Yeah, yeah, I'm sorry but there is gas! There is fucking gas!"

Dia sighed as he clasped onto Zach's shoulder.

"Listen man! You keep your mask on and you won't be dead! Alright? Gas is just part of the conflict! Alright?" Dia said sternly,

Zach nodded as he shivered, both from his own fear and as a result of the freezing temperatures of Saint Petersburg. His ragged breathing started to settle.

"Good boy, now do as I say, breathe…squeeze…kill…breathe again! Try that!"

Zach followed the instructions and actually managed to shut down a machine.

"That's it, boy! Keep that up. And you'll stay alive for longer!"

"Yeah, thanks, Dia!"

"Don't mention it, you are part of the team now so we have to keep you alive!"

CHAPTER 8: BATTLE IN SAINT PETERSBURG

In the distance, Zach could see the distinctive architecture of the Church of the Saviour on Spilled Blood. The fact that its colourful conical domes were still towering over the city meant that for now, the church which made Saint Petersburg stand out from the other Terran cities was still standing strong, untouched by the destructive power of modern weapons. However, all around, the city was quickly becoming a burning ruin. Huge volumes of smoke were rising into the sky. Looking around him, Zach could only look with horror at the wanton destruction. This was a place that many people called home, a place where people lived, worked, married and raised their children, just like Zach's family back in New York. He dreaded the possibility that such a battlefield could take place in his home city of New York.

Up in the sky, the battle was still taking place, as flying fortresses and frigates traded shots with each other. Fighter aircraft engaged in dogfights above the city. To support their comrades flying past them, the gunners on the flak turrets of the flying fortresses fired at the attacking drones. The crew of flying fortresses wore armour and visored, bone-dome helmets during a battle. A machine frigate swooped in at the *Tungsten* firing several missiles at it, blasting away turrets and killing their crews. The *Tungsten*, however, was not brought down by this and it continued to fight on.

On the bridge of the *Tungsten*, Rufus Thorne observed the ongoing battle on the ground via a holographic map. On the map, it was very clear that the machines were gaining the upper hand as the holographic map of Saint Petersburg was quickly turning red. The areas of green which symbolised the areas held by humanity were quickly fading away. Rufus looked on stoically, but deep in his mind he realised that the machine force was much more powerful and vicious than anticipated. He knew that the army was going to have to regroup and reorganise if they were going to stand a chance.

"Lord God, what a serious mess! The Black Mouth must be in the area, how else would they be showing this level of intelligence?" Jethro said to himself as Rufus approached.

"Colonel Jethro! The Legionnaires have new orders!" Rufus said.

"What are they to do sir?"

"Colonel Jethro, this battle is going ill, I am issuing a retreat!"

"   But what about the civilians, sir? The people that inhabit the city. We can't just leave them to die!"

"Colonel Jethro, they are to be evacuated with the troops as ordered but when that is done, I want the city destroyed!"

"The whole city of St Petersburg? This city was built by Tsar Peter the Great in 1703! Do you really want to go down in the canon as the one who obliterated several centuries of history?"

"Yes, the city is a key industrial facility that must be of no use to the enemy. We must have it bombed! History means nothing to those who are trying to preserve the future of our race!"

Jethro was horrified at this request, but he complied with the order. He prepared to send a message to the various commanders as the battle became more desperate.

* * *

Meanwhile back down in Saint Petersburg, the battle was still going on. By now the rest of the Legionnaires had caught up with Alpha Squad. Troops of tanks and armoured cars had arrived and the tracks of the tanks ground their way across the now ruined roads of Saint Petersburg, firing their turrets and blazing their guns in hope of clearing out any potential enemies. Inside the tank were its crew who were operating the controls in order to keep the vehicle moving and firing. The gunner was operating the tank's guns from a screen within his helmet. The kind of helmet that tankers wore looked like a virtual reality device. As a result, these tankers experienced the battle as if it were a video game, making them disconnected from the fight. Unlike the soldiers with their boots on the ground, they didn't experience the violence of war directly.

As he just knocked out an enemy tank, the gunner remarked in an amused tone, "Well guys, when I was a little one, I thought there were too many machines, now, I don't think there are enough! How things change when you are in a tank!"

The rest of the crew laughed.

"Yeah, mate, that won't be the case when a shell manages to take us out!" The driver responded sarcastically.

"Hey, keep on the pedal, we need to work together if we don't want that to happen…"

"Ah yeah, relax, man, you're all in safe hands!"

But the crew of that tank were unaware that a machine squad had taken cover among the ruins. As the tank rather jovially stampeded across the streets, those robots fired a rocket. It slammed straight into the side of the tank, knocking it out of action. Such scenarios were common throughout the city. Much further ahead in the streets, Alpha Squad was taking cover behind the ruins of a bus. Zach was slowly starting to get better at firing. This made him feel glad because it meant that he was finally becoming useful to his team. Beside him, Dermot was in the process of reloading his rifle when he got a wound in the cheek. Blood started to pour out of Dermot's cheek.

"Wait! Wait! are you okay?" Zach asked him,

Much to his surprise, Dermot quickly snapped out of his shocked position and mopped the blood off with his gloved hand.

"Don't worry! It's just a scratch!" Dermot replied.

He continued to snipe. The ruined bus they were behind was getting increasingly tattered, so the team prepared to move on to better cover, this time behind a wall. As they ran towards the wall a missile narrowly shot past the team, exploding in close proximity, knocking them to the ground. Zach fell to the ground and felt an immense surge of pain go through his body.

Fortunately, his augmented body was much tougher and as a result, he and the others were able to survive the explosion that occurred near him. However, the explosion of the missile had stirred up huge amounts of dust making it harder to see. During Zach's fall, a high-pitched noise went off in his ears, followed by swirling unstable imagery and distorted voices calling out to him. His eyes were sore as he struggled to get up. Machines were approaching his position, but they were taken out by a nearby tank that trundled straight past him. As he heaved himself up, he heard a voice.

"You're getting battered easily, little brother, aye?" It was Alexi.

"Yeah well!! I'm new to the fight! I'm not superman!" Zach was frustrated,

Alexi reached out to clasp Zach's hand and help him up.

"Don't worry, it happens to all of us in our youth! Trust me, we all went through this as well...so don't worry kid, being stomped isn't anything to be ashamed about when it's your first day!"

What Alexi said should have felt reassuring, but Zach found it hard to smile. While it was his first day in combat, there was an ugly chance that it could become the last day in his life. That was something Zach intended to avoid, no matter how gritty and dirty things went.

Back onto his own two feet, he managed to keep up with the team as they took cover behind the wall.

"Colonel Jethro, this is Captain Faulkner, we have just reunited with the other units...it's a mess, this battle is going ill! What the fuck just happened?" Michael said into his shoulder radio.

"Captain Faulkner, thank God you're alive... yes, the battle has gone ill...the machines have brought in heavy vehicles and tanks. You need to get the civilian population out of here, right now!"

"Are we in retreat, sir? What's going to happen to the city?"

"Yes, machine assault frigates and cruisers are already engaging our flying fortresses,
St Petersburg seems lost, but Rufus doesn't want the city to be useful for the machines, he's ordering a full carpet bombing of the city...but he wants to get all units and civilians out of the city before the bombardment commences!"

"Okay, we'll see what we can do, sir!"

"Thank God for that, Captain, because this has got to be one of the biggest messes that we've ever gotten into...Going to warn you, captain, the bombardment is starting very soon! I'm informing all other units to perform a general retreat!! Over."

"I understand sir! I'll see what we can do! Over and out!"

Michael sighed with pure despair. As far as he was concerned, the civilians were quite safe underground in their shelters but if Rufus gave an order, it had to be carried out. He then turned around to the rest of the team.

"Gentlemen! We've got new orders from Rufus Thorne! We're ordered to retreat! He is going to bombard the whole city of Saint Petersburg so that the machines can't use it to fuel their war effort!!"

All the men were dumbstruck by the thought that Rufus would bombard a city. Zach felt an ugly sense of dread. Such a decision painted Rufus in a very different light now. Vincent spoke.

"What? The whole city?? What about the little ones?? Does that Oxford don have any heart??"

"It's not as simple as that, we also have orders to evacuate the civilian population so that the city can be repopulated with its original inhabitants in the future! Is that understood?"

"Yes, sir!"

"Good gentlemen! Let's get this done!"

The squad joined with other regiments and squadrons as they headed back to the dropships.

* * *

What ensued was one of the most chaotic evacuations that the team had ever been a part of as the Legion covered the fleeing population. Wardens and Home Guard troops did their best to guide them to the dropships so that they could be evacuated. Dimitri did his best to keep up with his parents but in the confusion, he slipped and let go of his father's hand. Scared, he scrambled up, but he was unable to see his parents and he was soon lost among a sea of people. Shivers went up Dimitri's spine as he found himself alone among a crowd of strangers. Feeling alone, sad and terrified all at the same time, he cried out.

"Mum? Mum! Dad! Mum."

Nicholas heard his son's voice cry out. He realised he was no longer holding Dimitri's hand and couldn't see him anywhere.

"Nicholas?" Anya called to him.

"Anya? I..."

"Where's Dimitri? I thought you had him!"

"I know I thought I had him too...I"

Then, they heard Dimitri cry out for them. Turning around, Nicholas yelled out, "Dimitri!"

"Dad?"

"Stay there, we are coming! Stay calm!"

Nicholas and Anya had no qualms charging through the crowd to try to get to their son, but two Guardsmen stopped them. Desperate to get back to his son, Nicholas tried to push past them but he was powerless to break through the onrush of people behind him and he was pushed back towards the ramps of the dropship.

"Hey, you are going the wrong way!" One of them said to Nicholas.

"But our son is back there, we need to get him back! Let us past! Please sir!"

Despite the desperate and heart-wrenched expressions on both Nicolas's and Anya's faces the Guardsman wouldn't budge,

"Get back to the dropships!! The bombardment of the city is commencing in a few minutes! Now get back you idiots! Get back!"

Dimitri could only helplessly look on as his parents were pushed back away from him by the pressure of the crowd. Nearby, Zack and his teammates were fighting to hold back the machine advance. Zach noticed the boy running desperately towards the dropship as the ramp was raised, ready to take off.

Zach watched the boy slump down in despair as the dropship slowly rose. This stung his heart as he was reminded of his own experience. Unaware that Zach was observing him, the boy scrambled up and ran back towards the metro station because he didn't want to be in the heat of a battle where a shot from either side could get him killed. Zach could not stop looking after the boy as feelings of hopelessness and disruption within a family in a war zone was something Zach was all too painfully familiar with.

* * *

The battle went on and the flying fortresses managed to finally punch through the machine fleet, but one of the enormous vessels had been shot down, tumbling down in a ball of flames and exploding before it could reach the ground. The bombardment was already starting to commence; a hail of bombs was already beginning to fall on the city. Seeing more and more dropships start to take off, Zach thought of the boy he just saw. The look of terror on the boy's face was burnt into his mind and he couldn't get it out of his head. The rest of the squad was too busy fighting to even notice the child. With the majority of the civilian population and the Terran military presence evacuated, as far as Michael was concerned, it was time to go. As a result, he turned to his team and ordered them to evacuate.

Seeing Zach just standing and starring, Michael came over to him.

"Hey, Zach! Come on! We need to get out of here! The bombardment is going to start right now!"

However, having seen a boy getting separated from his parents, Zach asked, "Wait... that's not all the civilians? There's more!"

"We have no time...we searched everywhere. And there are no more civilians in the area!"

"But sir! There are still people out there! I swear I just saw a kid back there!"

Michael stared angrily at Zach. He grasped the younger man's shoulder.

"Zach, don't be foolish! the bombardment is commencing and once it is done, we are going straight back into the battle!! You have a life and a purpose! I lost Hans at Edinburgh; I'm not letting another trooper lose his life! Especially over a hallucination!"

However, the very thought of leaving someone for dead gave Zach ugly memories about how his father had been essentially left behind for dead by the wardens. He refused to allow another family to go through the same trauma.

Zach pushed Michael's arm off him.

"I'm a goner anyway, useless new meat, so I'm going after him!! I thought the aim of the Terran state was to preserve life!"

Michael was stunned.

"Zach! Don't be irrational!!"

Zach ran off into the city that was being bombarded and battered by the flying fortresses as they desperately cleansed the place of machines. He headed for the metro station where he had last seen the boy. Machine hordes were being wiped out in a grand scale by this bombardment, so they also called a retreat. The machines retreated their assets with the hope of taking over the area once the bombardment had been completed. Only then would they return and establish a base in the area from which to punch into Europe.

Zach didn't stop to think about whether what he was doing was impractical or not. He was driven by an urge to find that child. He may have been powerless when he was a little boy but now, he had the enhancements and he had a gun, he had power and he wanted to use it for good.

Behind him, Dermot and Michael were locked in a furious argument. Dermot was yelling in desperation.

"Zach!! ZACH!!!! COME BACK!!! COME BACK WE DON'T WANT YOU DEAD!!"

"Don't!! It's useless...I'll try to contact him by radio!!" Michael cut across him.

"But he'll be considered a deserter! You might have to kill him if he doesn't comply! I don't want to have to see a young lad his age die like that!"

"I know!! That's why I'm going to try and call him back!"

Dermot stopped. By now, the bombardment was coming to an end and the whole city of Saint Petersburg was a smoking ruin. Even if it slowed down the machine advance, the ruins of Saint Petersburg were an unpleasant sight for the sore eyes of war weary Legionnaires. Alpha Squad was now the only squad of Legionnaires remaining in the area. They returned to their dropship where Alonzo was waiting. Seeing his comrades return, he noticed that Zach wasn't there.

"Eh sir? Wasn't there seven of you? Where is Zach, Captain?" He said to Michael.

In a harsh and saddened tone, Michael responded.

"He's not with us, Alonzo."

Alonzo felt an icy shock go up his spine.

"Sweet Jesus!! What has happened to him? Is he dead, sir?"

"No, he's lost! The fool went delusional! He claimed that there was a child still in the street, but he was probably hallucinating!"

"Are there any orders for us, sir?"

Michael paused before replying.

"For now, we wait here! I'll try to contact Zach! If he doesn't respond...I'll go and shoot him myself! Is that understood?"

"Yes, sir!"

The team waited by the dropship.

CHAPTER 9: THE LOST CHILD

Zach crept deep into the old subways of St Petersburg. The pitch-black subways were not a comfortable place to be around. But he had a job to do, that child was still out there somewhere. As Zach continued his journey down into the metro station, he felt his shoulder radio beeping. It was Michael.

"Zach...where are you? Zach...you got to get out of there.... Zach, are you even listening to me? Zach? The machines are closing in now as we speak...Zach??"

But Zach turned off the radio after saying, "I'm sorry, Captain, but I am not giving up on this kid."

He looked at his scanner which had a beeping spot flashing red. This gave him hope because red meant warmth, and warmth meant life. Curious, he pressed on, lighting his way with the spotlight attached to his gun.

***

Back at the dropship, Michael, now angry and furious, slammed his fist against the dropship's hull as he snapped

"Damn the stupid boy...got too overconfident...too curious...it's going to be the death of him!!"

"Well, you have to admire him in some way...to explore a city that is very possibly going to be under machine control soon...you kind of need some serious balls to do that, sir!" Alexi replied.

"MAYBE HE HAS BALLS, ALEXI!! BUT HE HAS NO BRAINS!"

Alexi went quiet as Michael turned around to look him in the eyes. He sighed in despair. He was furious at Zach not because he hated the youth but precisely because he cared about Zach and didn't want him to die.

Hearing this, Chang approached the two men. For all their initial resentment they felt towards the young rookie, neither Chang, Alexi nor Dia nor even Vincent wanted to see Zach dead. For if each new squad member died, the circle would just go on.

With this in mind, Chang spoke to Michael,

"Michael, Dia and I can go look for the boy. If he is a new meat, then he is at his most vulnerable. It won't be long before some sort of horror descends upon him!"

Michael looked back to the men as they had their eyes fixed on him.

"Gentlemen," Michael began, "I admire your sympathy, but this is on me. The rest of you stay by the dropship. No matter how intense it gets you are to stay as a team. We can't risk losing any more of you. Am I understood?"

"Yes, sir!"

The others started to dig in and fortify around the dropship as Michael then went off muttering to himself.

"Damn, always the seventh squad member. Hans got killed, now Zach has got lost... it all makes sense...why ancient cultures saw seven as an unlucky number."

* * *

Deep in the underground station, Zach's heart was thumping as he advanced with his gun at the ready. He heard a noise as if something was moving. He kept his finger very firmly on the trigger so that if he heard a single noise around him, he would have his weapon at the ready. He was painfully aware of the fact that was alone in the middle of a ruined landscape. He raised his scanner to check it and found that it was still beeping and flashing red. However, the flashing was getting quicker and quicker as an indication that the lifeform, whatever it was, was getting closer and closer to him.

Zach raised his rifle again, aiming it ahead of him as he moved through the corridors of the subway. The noises all around him were most likely the sound of rats and other creatures that made their home in the tunnels. For now, he still felt a moment of dread, sheer dread. However, when he identified the source of the noises he had heard, he stopped. He knelt down, lowered his rifle and, much to his shock and awe, he saw the little boy. Closer, the boy looked only to be between six or seven, huddled in a corner. The boy had dirt and grease on him, he had short blonde hair and blue eyes. He seemed to have a small furry coat and a pair of gloves on him. Covering the boy's lower body were soft trousers and furry boots. He was huddled up in fear against a corner. Zach approached the little boy, but the child merely scrambled further and further into the corner. Zach tried to raise his hand as if to show the boy that he was not going to harm him. At first Zach seemed confused as to why the boy was afraid of him but then it suddenly dawned on him, both his gas mask and his helmet obscured his facial features and probably made him look like some sort of machine or robot. Realising that his very appearance was scaring the boy, Zach took off both his gas mask and his helmet. He then lightly touched the boy on the shoulder.

"Hey little guy, what's your name? I'm not a machine, I'm Zach."

The boy seemed to look a lot more comforted by seeing Zach's face, but he continued to huddle.

"Mum? Dad? Where's my Mum?" The boy said in Russian.

Zach didn't really know how to hold a conversation in Russian, but he could figure out that the boy was probably looking for his parents.

This was a reality Zach was all too familiar with since the battle of New York. Zach thought about what to do. He certainly wouldn't leave this child behind in the darkness at the mercy of the machines, but he didn't really know where the child's parents were taken. Still, he knew what he had to do so he slowly approached and, as gently and as reassuringly as possible, he spoke to the boy.

"Hey, little guy, I'm sorry but I don't know where your Mum is but tell you what, I'll try and get you back to her, okay? But even though I can't promise you that., you're going to have to trust me. Okay?"

The boy seemed confused and disorientated but he nodded. However, movement could be heard behind Zach and a spotlight was shining on the new meat's back. Zach didn't turn around, but he was sure it was Michael behind him, for he had become very familiar with the brooding presence of his commander.

Feeling the rage that was radiated by Michael's presence, Zach spoke in a quiet but angry tone.

"Captain Michael Faulkner, I presume?"

As he approached Zach from behind, Michael aimed his rifle.

"You know, you just ran off on my squad in the heat of battle for the sake of glory and on the basis of delusions…and then when I try to call you back…you ignored my calls! That in most armies, including this one, would merit an execution. So, are you coming back with us, or do I have to kill you?"

Zach maintained his frown and breathed in, lifting Dimitri into his arms.

"By all means Captain. I'm a new meat. I'm useless to your squad of experts. By all means shoot me!!" He replied sarcastically.

Michael raised his rifle and placed his finger on the trigger. He tried to bring himself to push the trigger, but he found that even with all the rage he couldn't bear to kill one of his own squad so soon after the death of Hans. However, it seemed to him that there was no convincing Zach to come back, so he readied his finger.

But, before Michael could fire his gun, Zach turned around to face him, exposing the boy to the spotlight of Michael's gun.

"Because I thought the Legion's goal was to preserve life," Zach continued, "not leave it at the mercy of the machines!! Are you going to shoot the child as well??"

The little boy's frightened face suddenly filled Michael with shock. Suddenly his anger started to melt away. He breathed in and lowered his rifle.

"So that's why you ditched us, because of this child, a foolish and irrational act yes but you did it not out of a foolish thirst for grandiosity but out of empathy. Where did you find this boy? What's his name?"

"I don't know his name, but I found him hiding here in the metro. Michael, he's a civilian, and a vulnerable little guy like me! As a result, I don't intend to leave him here!"

Seeing how small and young the boy looked, Michael responded.

"We are not adding him to 'Team Orca'!! He is but a child!!

Where are his parents?" He said sternly.

"I don't know, but I was briefly near a dropship evacuating civilians, and I saw two civilians, one male and one female, both pretty young, but they seemed to be wondering about someone they called Dimitri. They were boarded onto the dropship, but they must have lost their child, and I've just found him."

Michael looked on with concern. He thought for a while, before placing his hand on Zach's shoulder.

"Tell you what? We take this boy with us. The civilians were being evacuated to refugee camps in Norway. They will wait at these camps until the Legion has retaken the city and secured the area around it. Then they will repopulate the city with its original inhabitants. This is something we do with every human region, regardless of who they are and what they worship!"

"Do you think that the kid's parents will be waiting for him there, Sir?"

"Of course, they will. We'll try to get him there because that's all he wants, his parents. It should only take a few hours by dropship. Is that alright?"

Zach felt a surge of relief and gratitude that Michael was willing to spare time to get the child back to his parents.

"Thank you, sir, I am grateful that you are willing to spare the time to get this kid home!"

"Alright Zach. Your act may not seem that much on the grander scale but every victory and very life saved counts!"

Zach closed his eyes briefly. His earlier anger towards Michael and the rest of the team was starting to fade away. He suddenly started to remember all the moments in the battle in which a member of the team saved his life. Such actions overshadowed the earlier mistreatment that some of the men had subjected him too. He smiled to himself. He was going back to his team.

CHAPTER 10: ESCAPE FROM SAINT PETERSBURG

Up on the surface, the rest of the team were waiting by the dropship. Alonzo paced beside his vehicle while the others stayed at the ready. Vincent held his machine gun close to him. Chang and Alexi had their weapons positioned on rubble so that they would be ready to respond, however they played cards to pass the time. Dermot kept an eye out, observing the surrounding environment with his binoculars with his sniper rifle at the ready. Alonzo was starting to feel frustrated by the long wait. They were in the middle of enemy territory and they were on their own. He knew that at any moment the machines could attack them, and they wouldn't last long in such conditions. Plus, the sun was already starting to go down. Alonzo was afraid that Rufus Thorne might think of them as dead or worse, he might get the impression that they had deserted.

"Dermot? Any sign of Captain Faulkner?"

"No, Alonzo, he must be still down there in the subway!"

Alonzo slammed his fist against the hull of his dropship in frustration.

"Damn it! Guys, we should get out of here!"

The men simply looked back at Alonzo. They were in no position to move while their leader was out there in the ruined wasteland of Saint Petersburg.

"What did you just say, Alonzo?" Vincent asked.

"You heard me! I'm going to start the engine; we can't say here!"

"Are you asking us to leave Michael? Fuck off! He is our leader!"

"Damn it, Vincent! We are in the middle of enemy territory; the machines will be coming here to claim this place! The longer we stay here, the higher the risk of annihilation! If we leave, we can reach the *Tungsten*, we can arrange with Jethro to organise a search party!"

However, the team all looked at him oddly.

"What is wrong with you guys?"

There was a cold silence as the team glared angrily at Alonzo but then Chang butted in.

"Alonzo, we are aware of the circumstances that we find ourselves in, but we cannot afford to just abandon Michael. He's our leader and he would go back for anyone of us. He's just gone back for our new boy!"

Alonzo sighed.

"Okay, I get it, he's your boss. Yeah, he's my boss as well but what if he is dead? Why hasn't he contacted us? I just want to do my job in keeping you lot safe! Flying you in and out of zones is how I do it!"

"We are aware of your concern and we thank you for it. I suggest we try contacting Michael for an update." Dia said.

Alonzo jumped up onto the ramp.

"Stay here! I'll establish contact with him via the cockpit. Keep an eye out for machines."

"Understood, Alonzo!"

Alonzo went to the cockpit of the dropship. It was slightly comforting to feel the warmth of the cockpit after the chill outside. Reactivating the control panel, he reached for the radio so that he could call Michael.

* * *

Outside the dropship, the team continued to wait. Dermot continued to observe the surrounding area of the city. The once beautiful city of St Petersburg now looked like a tattered ruin, many of the buildings now unrecognisable as they had been reduced to mere rubble. The burning wrecks of the vehicles had been stripped of all their colours as a result of the fire. The wires of the tramlines still streaked across the city. Even the churches and their golden domes had been battered by the bombardment. So determined was Rufus that the machines could never reap the benefits of any victory that he was ready to sacrifice entire cities worth of monuments and centuries of culture. Its saddened Dermot to see the sight but there was one source of comfort.

That was that the people were mostly evacuated so their culture would live on in them. They knew how the city was supposed to look so with Terran engineering they could recreate the city in its proper image. Dermot noticed a spot in the air. It was coming faster and faster towards the team and their dropship. Concerned, Dermot zoomed his binoculars to it. His eyes widened and he yelled

"Drone!!!!"

The rest of the team scrambled to their positions. The drone was heading for the dropship. Seeing this, Dia shouted into his radio.

"Alonzo! Get out of there! There is a drone coming!"

"What? Okay, I'm coming…"

The drone let out a wailing noise with its siren as it swooped down towards the dropship. Alonzo dropped the radio and fled the cockpit but just as he emerged into the cargo bay, the drone dropped its bombs.

All the men ducked as the dropship got blown up, taking Alonzo with it. The loss of both the dropship and Alonzo in one go shook the men with horror and sadness. Dermot yelled.

"Alonzo!!!"

Alexi slowly made the sign of the cross, not just because they had just lost Alonzo, but because they were now facing the ugly reality that they had very little chance of reuniting with the *Tungsten* now. To make things worse, they were in the middle of enemy territory and the machines were coming in quick.

Robotic soldiers were coming towards them. Mostly these were just infantry armed with the standard armour piercing assault rifles. However suddenly, bursting out of the ground were at least two robotic spiders. These spiders were bristling with both machine guns, grenade launchers and buzz saws. They scuttled towards the team very quickly.

"Alert! Machines coming! Many of them! They even have spider bots!!" Dermot shouted.

Hearing this, Dia ordered the group.

"Alright boys! You heard Dermot, take cover and ready your weapons!"

The team prepared for the oncoming onslaught. Dia, knowing that Michael was still out there, activated his shoulder radio to contact Michael. The battle had already begun, and the team were firing their guns, forcing the machines to take cover.

* * *

Meanwhile, down in the metro station, Michael's shoulder radio flashed red. Michael pressed on it to respond.

"Come in?"

In the background, Michael could hear gunfire and shouting as Dia's voice yelled into the radio.

"Captain Faulkner, sir, this is Dia, do you copy?"

Hearing the sound of gunfire through the radio caused Michael's eyes to widen with dread.

"Talk to me, Dia?"

"Captain...we've lost our dropship; we're barely holding out...Alonzo is dead! Captain, do you copy?"

Michael's face went pale with shock. It was an ugly surprise for Michael to learn that not only was the dropship destroyed but that Alonzo was killed as well. This had just made their mission of returning the boy to his parents much more difficult to accomplish.

"Hold on, Zach and I are coming...we've got a child with us."

"You've got a kid with you? How's that going to help?"

"Listen, Dia, it's complicated but we are coming! Over and out!"

When the radio transmission ended, Michael turned around to Zach.

"Zach, get your headgear and mask back on...you're going to need it!!"

Zach fitted on his equipment. He felt shocked and horrified over what he had heard through the radio,

"Did our dropship just get destroyed, sir?"

"Yes, it did! Now, come along Zach, no time to waste!"

Zach felt a vicious surge of guilt in his heart when he heard the news. He knew that the reason that the dropship got destroyed was because it didn't just fly away like the other dropships. The team had waited for him because they cared for him and this had put the whole team in grave danger. He picked up Dimitri and followed Michael out of the subway.

* * *

Back in the dropship, the team were holding out beside the ruined ship, taking out any machine that came close. Their network of fortifications was successful enough to hold out against the robotic onslaught. Michael and Zach emerged from the subway, running and dodging any robotic patrols that were patrolling the city. At long last, they were able to reunite with the squad. Under the cover of Dermot's sniper fire, they made their way back to the other sides of the entrenchments.

After a prolonged battle, the machines retreated. Zach let go of Dimitri and let him sit down beside him. The rest of the team looked at them.

"Well, you came back, sir, praise God for your return!" Alexi said.

"God? Alexi, God has abandoned this place. We survived out of dumb luck."

Seeing Dimitri, the little boy that was beside Zach, Alexi asked Zach, "Who's that?"

"He's a kid I found in the subway. He got separated from his parents during the battle. I'm sorry."

"Why are you sorry, boy? You went on a suicide mission to find that kid. He's one of my people, you know." Alexi replied.

Zach sighed as he stood up. His response was sad and sorrowful,

"It's just that...it's because my actions made you all wait for me. And such an act led to the death of your pilot. I know I came here to this unit because your previous mate, Hans had died in battle! And now, I barely knew Alonzo…but I'm sorry that he died."

Zach clasped his gloved hand against his face but then much to his surprise, the team came over to him in a comforting manner. Chang even put his hand on Zach's shoulder.

"Zach…no…," Chang began, "you may have been the one who went into the subway. But it is us who choose to stay here. If we really all hated you, we would have just taken off without you. We all stayed here because both you and Michael were still behind. It may be irrational to stay behind, but that is the Terran way."

The team went to work on the wreckage of the dropship, tearing through it so as to haul out Alonzo's scorched body. They then laid the burnt corpse on the ground, surrounding Alonzo with flammable material. Kneeling down, Michael used his lighter to set the debris and the body alight, cremating Alonzo so that he could reach the afterlife. There was no time for a full-on ritual. Nevertheless, the death of their pilot and their long-time comrade wasn't taken lightly by the team. They all circled around Alonzo.

They held their helmets in their hands as they all looked solemnly and silently at the burning body. Dermot, Alexi and Michael made the sign of the cross. The sparks of the fire rose up into the increasingly darkening sky. Zach had barely known who Alonzo was, but his death still chilled him. He could still sense the grief that the men had for their fallen pilot. It was a cruel reminder that this war, or any war before it, cared for no one. It mattered little who you were, only that you could be killed at any moment.

***

Some time had passed, and the sky was getting even darker. Dermot approached Michael.

"Captain Faulkner! What the bloody hell do we do now?"

Looking at the tattered remains of the dropship, Michael thought for a while before he spoke,

"Well, we can use our radios to stay in contact with each other…but we have no radio now to call home. We'll be too small to pick up on the scanners of any of the flying fortresses…according to our GPS…the nearest uplink from here is at the southern edge of the Arctic Circle. It's not too far from here but we will have to cross

Badlands."

"And how do we cross them, Captain? The Badlands are known to be the place of monsters, mutated beasts produced from freak experiments; machines also patrol the place. We could even come across the Black Mouth on its warpath. We would have no chance!"

"What can I say? Am I going to lie to the lot of you that we have teleporters?"

Hearing this question, the team shook their heads.

"Well then...we have no choice...but to go by foot! So that's what we are doing!! Now if you want to stay behind and wait for the next robotic war party or dropship...that's fine...any volunteers?"

They all shook their heads.

"Good! Let's move on!" Michael said,

The team moved on. Zach was still carrying Dimitri since the boy probably couldn't keep up with the genetically enhanced men even if he was running on his own two feet. On seeing the little boy, Vincent spoke.

"Zach...who is that?"

"A little boy...separated from his parents, I decided to take him under my wing until we can bring him back to his parents!"

"Aye, good boy...keep the little one safe...if he dies it'll be on your head...so grow some balls...one to keep that boy alive...two to kick some mechanical asses...three to give a good explanation to mama bear if you fail to protect her cub!"

"Vincent come on...we don't have time for this; besides, Zach may be a boy, but his body has been enhanced and modified to fight, I'm sure the boy will be fine anyway." Chang snapped.

"Alright Chang...but hold up for Zach...he's got a kid with him."

As the team moved on, Zach looked up at the sky. He could see some of the flying fortresses still hovering in the distance. He hoped that they might eventually be able to spot them so that they could send a dropship to retrieve them and get Dimitri back to his parents. However, the flying fortresses were continuing the offensive in other regions; it was as if they didn't notice them.

"Hey, Zach, come on...we need to get going..." Alexi said, tapping him on the shoulder.

Zach turned around to follow the group. Behind him, he could hear the sounds of the bombardment that was already taking place. As he walked away, Zach wondered if he would ever get used to the sound of such ordnance, despite the fact that it was a sound he was all too familiar with, even before he ended up in the Terran military.

CHAPTER 11: THE LANDS CURSED BY WAR

Rufus Thorne stood in the control room of the Tungsten, observing the holographic map. The Legion was starting to regroup so that they could continue the offensive and press on across the Russian Steppes up to the Ural Mountains. Jethro entered through the door and approached him.

"Have all the civilians been evacuated safely, Colonel?" Rufus asked Jethro.

"Yes, sir! The dropships are heading to Trosmo!"

"Good, cities are just cities, protecting the people is always key to preserving a region's culture, not the buildings. For the buildings can always be rebuilt. Anyway, how about our legions, Colonel, are they safe?"

"The majority of our legions been evacuated but we suffered heavy casualties! One squad got left behind, sir."

"What? A squad got left behind?? Any squad in particular, Colonel?"

"Alpha Squad, sir...we've had no contact from their dropship...Commander!"

Until then, the officers in the control room had been following their usual routines and observing the holographic screens. When they heard the news that Alpha Squad was missing, the men stopped what they were doing and went silent. The very news that their finest squad was missing stunned them. Everyone in the room, including the guards, looked at Rufus. Rufus also went silent in horror, taking off his peaked cap and placing his hand on the handle by the holographic map.

"They were our finest squad. They are probably dead, knowing them. They risk their lives so irrationally no matter what the order is." He said to himself in a whisper.

Jethro cleared his throat and asked, "Commander, what are our orders?"

"Colonel Jethro!" he began, recovering his composure, "If

they are alive then they will most likely be heading through the Badlands, lost, trying to find an uplink. A savage place riddled with machines and genetic monstrosities! A no man's land that lies between Terra and the machine industrial complex! There are so many abominations there that it will take the logistic capacity of a flying fortress to successfully sustain a search party in this region. You will inform the *Valiant* of this recent update. They will perform a search party starting in Saint Petersburg and going up into the Badlands to search for the team! Am I understood?"

"Yes, sir! I will inform the captain of the *Valiant* right away!"

Followed by an officer, Jethro used the radio on the Tungsten to relay the order to the flying fortress *Valiant*. Upon receiving the order, the *Valiant* flew off on its mission. The enormous behemoth of a flying fortress shined its lights as it trekked into the dark wintery night. The howling winds and hails of snow had no effect on the *Valiant* and its crew.

* * *

The wind howled violently over the Badlands, a stretch of territory in the North of Europe rendered uninhabitable for humans. The land itself was stripped barren by heavy bombardment from flying fortresses and bombers on both sides. It was icy, and snow covered the land. Old Russian and European military bases littered the Badlands; these bases were filled with old war equipment, and robots very often scavenged there for fuel and munitions. If you were lucky, you might find an old uplink through which they could communicate to the nearest flying fortress and signal to them your location.

This is exactly where the team was, including Dimitri. The team had to survive on their rations which they shared with the boy. Fortunately, as they were a race of superhumans, most of the team could survive for longer periods without starving or being thirsty. Still, they were scavenging spare food when they could. They kept their weapons at the ready as other kinds of lifeforms dwelt here: monsters that were the product of genetic experiments during the Third World War, creatures that were now lurking in the wilderness. They were stronger and tougher than normal animals, and they were more aggressive and vicious.

The thunder of the flying fortress bombardment could be heard in the distance as the grand offensive began. Looking back, Vincent spoke.

"I have to admit Alexi, I feel guilty for not taking part in that offensive. The boys are going to be wondering if we deserted or not."

"Yes, that could be the case, but we don't have the means. Our dropship was destroyed! We need to get to the nearest uplink!"

"And we have that kid."

"Yeah, true, but we were all kids once, Vincent."

At the same time, Zach was speaking to Dia.

"How long to go? We've been in this wasteland for days!"

"I don't know, we've probably have covered more land than we think!"

"How do you know?"

"It feels long because we are used to dropships, but, trust me, we're probably here for less time than we think!"

The team continued through the billowing blizzard till an old Russian military base came into view.

It seemed as if the team were in luck, as the base was a well-fortified facility guarded by observation posts, and it had an array of old military vehicles such as tanks, armoured personnel carriers, trucks and even helicopters. It also had a wide array of handguns and anti-aircraft guns. The team spent time investigating the base to search for supplies such as food. It was decided that they would spend the night there.

* * *

That night, Zach sat by the campfire trying to warm himself. It was the first time that he had experienced such a cold climate because when the harsh winters hit back at home he and his family went underground. He shivered in the cold air of the abandoned military base.

"You don't fare well in the cold, do you, boy?" Dia asked him from behind.

"It's quite a different world from Africa, don't you think, Dia?" Zach remarked, pulling his hands away from the blaze of the campfire.

"Yeah, I know, I remember from experience, I was used to the heat back in Nigeria so when I was a new meat, deployed in Northern Europe, my bones couldn't stop rattling from the cold, so I constantly asked my friends when we were going back to the dropship. Have to admit, you're handling the cold a little bit better than I did."

"Am I?"

"Don't worry kid, you'll get used to it, you'll grow to like the people here as well. They are rough but they are hardy, and they are good folk once you get to know them."

Dia then walked off while Zach looked over at a sleeping Dimitri and smiled to himself.

❋ ❋ ❋

The following day, Dermot was on watch. He noticed something in the air while peering through his binoculars. His eyes widened at the sight because swooping down towards them were three fighter drones, shaped in a triangular shape, equipped with two miniguns and some missiles.

"Sir!! We have a troop of drones incoming and they are coming fast to our position!" Dermot yelled at Michael.

"Boys!! Bogeys incoming...take cover!" Michael yelled as he looked up at them.

The team rushed to the warehouse for cover as the drones fired some missiles and strafed the base, shredding through the walls and causing some fuel tanks to go off, destroying some of the helicopters in the base.

"Hey little guy...you're going to have to trust us, little buddy, ...alright?" Zach said, as he put Dimitri down.

Dimitri nodded then pointed behind Zach, as if trying to divert his attention to something.

"Any plans, Captain?" Zach asked Michael.

"Probably what the boy was thinking. Behind us is an old Russian anti-aircraft tank from World War 3...we're going to use it...you stay here with the kid. I, Chang and Dermot are going to use that device!"

"What about us? Sir!" Vincent asked.

"There's another flack vehicle behind you. You, Dia and Alexi will get into that!"

"Roger that captain! Come on, fellas, let's get to that truck!"

In the anti-aircraft tank, Chang drove while Michael and Dermot handled the heavy machine guns of the craft. Meanwhile, Alexi drove the flack truck while Dia and Vincent handled the anti-aircraft gun that was mounted on the vessel. Dermot rotated the turret of the tank to aim it at the drones as they came hurtling towards him. As soon as a drone got close, he blazed the turret's machine guns, which ripped through the lead drone causing it to crash. Another drone got its wing damaged by Dia and Vincent's gun, causing it to crash into the ice. The last drone relayed a message to its controller.

"Alert! Alert! Calling central command! I am facing heavy resistance from primitive technology...require immediate support! It is manned by Legionnaires!"

Two larger drones packed with bombs and missiles came swooping in. They had a cylindrical shape with long wings extending out on either side of the craft. As they came flying towards the battlefield, one of them spoke in a deep voice.

"Understood!"

The drones let out a wailing scream with their siren, which alerted Vincent and Dia to rotate their AA gun to fire at the drones. However, the bullets barely made a dent in these drones. Looking at each other, the two leapt off their truck. Alexi also got out. All three ducked as a drone dropped a bomb on their truck, destroying it. Meanwhile, Michael desperately tried to drive the tank out of the way of the blast, but it caught fire. Sensing the smell, Dermot got out of the vehicle and tried to extinguish the flames with a fire extinguisher, but the drone fired its machine gun, while its bullets bounced off his armour, managing to pierce the fire extinguisher.

"Abandon tank!" Dermot yelled.

Michael and Chang had already got the message and scrambled out of the tank as it burned, the fire getting more violent as the two climbed out. Another drone swooped in, firing a missile at the tank, blowing it up, sending the team rushing back towards the warehouse for cover once more. Seeing this, Zach and Dimitri got to where the team had left their equipment and grabbed the missile launcher. They went into the control room and aimed it up to the sky.

"Hey, ...help me hold this up...I'll have some difficulty aiming this properly!" Zach said to Dimitri as he felt the painful strain of the weapon on his shoulder.

Although Dimitri was a bit baffled, he and Zach managed to lift up the chunky weapon. As he peered up through the targeting device, Zach spoke to him.

"Come on, that's it, come on, shoot!"

In a burst of adrenaline, Zach pulled the trigger of the weapon, firing a missile out from the launcher. The missile was a direct hit, damaging the tail wing of the incoming drone, causing it to spiral into the warehouse and crash. The burning body of the machine slid into an old fuel tank, blowing it up. The other drone retreated away from the scene. Zach sighed with relief as they went to re-join the others. The rest of the team was speechless as they saw Zach and Dimitri come back with the rocket launcher.

"That's my rocket launcher, what are you doing with it?" Alexi asked.

"Sorry for stealing your weapon, but we were putting it to good use! Alexi, you guys were getting creamed by those drones, we couldn't allow that to happen."

"Good boy! I'll let you off this time because you saved our necks."

"Thanks, Alexi."

Zach let out a weary smile as he handed Alexi back his launcher.

"Wait, he took out that drone?" Vincent asked Alexi,

surprised.

"Yes, that's right, Vincent, Zach took down that drone!"

"Well, I have to admit that merits a drink!"

There was laughter all around. However, Zach still felt wary

* * *

The team continued on foot through the icy, barren landscape, leaving the tattered remains of the Russian military warehouse behind.

As they made their way from the base and went further North, Michael kept an eye on his compass as he led the team onwards.

"Dermot, aren't we going to scavenge a truck?" Zach asked Dermot.

"No...not as advantageous as you would think!"

"Why? They speed up the journey! They'd give our feet a rest."

"Aye, they do...but they are very easy targets, especially for drones to take pot shots at. They would also run out of fuel pretty quickly!"

"Won't we be more vulnerable on foot?"

"Somewhat but it will be easier to take cover on foot."

Zach asked no more questions. He had a strange feeling of being freezing cold, yet he was sweating as he carried his heavy load of equipment like the rest of them did. Everything, his backpack, his helmet and his rifle, made his entire body ache under the pressure of carrying them. Dimitri walked alongside him, having recuperated some of his energy. Feeling his lips go dry, Zach took out his flask to take a drink. He continued to gulp it down until Alexi grasped his wrist to stop him.

"What?" Zach said.

"Don't gulp down all your water, Zach, it's the hardest thing to come by in the Badlands so save it for when you really need it."

"Sorry..."

"Listen, Zach I'm only trying to teach you some tips. We've all been in your shoes before."

Zach stayed with the group but kept his distance from Vincent, unaware that Vincent was feeling both troubled and guilty about the way he had treated Zach earlier when they were on the flying fortress.

✲ ✲ ✲

That night, the group settled around a campfire, their laughter echoing across the night sky. Zach was trying to get to sleep, Dimitri was already fast asleep. Alexi got the beans ready to be cooked over the campfire. Vincent looked over at Zach.

"Vincent? Are you alright?" Dermot asked him.

"Dermot, shouldn't we let the boy come over here? He looks lonely."

"I'd say he's tired, Vincent, tired and homesick. He'll need to sleep."

"But Dermot, it's not just that. Oh, guys..."

"What is it, Vincent?" Dia butted in.

"It's that I've been an absolute jerk towards that boy! Seriously I tried to shoo him off, brawled Dermot over him, mocked his love for his mummy, treated him like crap. God, I'm sorry, since Hans's death, I've been acting like a dick!"

"I know, we treated him harshly, we all have. The war has ruined our consciences."

"But he's going to distance himself from me tomorrow again. I know it. He hates me boys. And with good reason."

"Maybe you could approach the boy, if you just admit what you've done, he'll understand. A simple set of kind words can mend serious damage."

"But he's a boy with a family, something none of us are."

"I know, we can thank whoever built the Black Mouth for that. I know that if it weren't for the machines, I'd be tending to a farm in Nigeria. I can barely remember my life as a boy. Our whole town got attacked by the machines. I was the only survivor...I learned to survive in the jungle, it was there that a Legionnaire battalion found me. They took me in as one of their recruits."

"And then you got shipped with us, Alpha Squad."

"Yep, Dermot, we all came from different regiments. Alpha Squad was the first regiment to represent various different Terran regions. Most regiments represented a continent."

Eventually, the beans were ready to be eaten.

"So, should we wake that boy up?" Alexi asked.

"It's best not to, Alexi, he's exhausted."

"But what about the little one?"

The team paused when Alexi asked that question.

"You mean Dimitri? He's fast asleep as well." Dermot asked eventually.

"I'm glad we picked him up. He's a Russian like me, all of you have experienced air raids, naval bombardments, attacks but we experience the bulk of the machine offensives in their full brutality. All of these Badlands were what made up the North of Russia and they were once teeming with life and woodlands. Yet we fight, even when it is hopeless; we just fight for our lands to be free!"

"Aye, you Slavs have a history of doing that, like us Scotsmen, hard not to find a tribe of humans that doesn't have a history of doing that. Not even a soft effete pacifist could 'educate' that primal instinct out of us, Terra is smart enough not to try...' Dermot introjected, much to the group's amusement.

Alexi then started yelling, and mimed the act of waving a sword, which made the group laugh. Finished, Dermot and he clinked been cans and fist-pumped as Alexi said,

"There is much that our two cultures share, Dermot! That is why we make a good team."

The group continued to goof and laugh till they eventually went to sleep. They kept as close to the fire as possible so as to warm their bodies as much as possible in the cold.

CHAPTER 12: NIGHT ATTACK

Zach tried hard to get to sleep but he couldn't. The events of the day made him very stimulated. He looked at Dimitri sleeping with his head on his lap. The little boy breathed slowly. Zach put his hand on the boy's chest so that he could hear the pleasant thumping of a normal human heart. Zach had difficulty understanding why a cute little boy like Dimitri and a nineteen-year-old like himself were among a bunch of strong muscular hunks that had seen war for as long as they could remember. Vincent appeared beside them.

"Zach?"

"What?"

"Still awake?"

"I am! Why are you concerned about my wellbeing all of a sudden?"

"Look, Zach....I need to talk to you now."

"At this hour of the night, really?? We'll wake up the boys."

"Can you at least let me speak?"

Zach stood up, wondering what the man who had until then been a brutish and aggressive soldier suddenly wanted to talk to him about. They went a little away from the campfire.

"So, what do you want from me? You've been nothing but an asshole to me since I joined the team...even when the others started to develop respect...you kept seeing me as a little twerp because I may not be a big hunk who's taken down fifty robots by myself, is that it?"

"Zach, come on buddy, just relax and let me explain! I've been trying to tell you this ever since we left St Petersburg...but you've been ignoring me for most of the journey!"

"Okay...you've got my attention now...what do you want to tell me?"

"Zach....since you joined our team, I have been nothing but a complete asshole to you. I get it Zach...I can figure out what you are thinking. Why should you look out for me...or even care about what happens to me? Every quality I've displayed towards you is exactly what a brother shouldn't be. Honestly, I'm surprised you didn't just drop out on us. The blunt truth, Zach is that I wasn't ready to take in another teammate. Hans and I, we've fought back-to-back since we were boys......since we were in the Legion...and I would have died for him...because he risked his life for me. His death caused me more damage and pain than if I had been coated with lime."

Zach paused, amazed by this confession.

"Well...what caused you to change your mind about me?"

"Zach, not many rookies would have just stopped to pick up one little boy, most would have probably just walked on...but you didn't. You may not be the best foot soldier...but you know how to be a brother."

Zach was quite deeply touched. He never thought that such a brute like Vincent could be capable of compassion. The two shook each other's gloved hands and locked eyes with each other as a sign of reconciliation. Then they returned to the campfire. As they looked down at a sleeping Dimitri. Vincent spoke again,

"What actually drove you to save that kid?"

"That kid is life, Vincent. I saw life get destroyed when I lost my father; I grew up without a father. This kid got separated from his parents during the battle for St Petersburg. When my father died, all I could do was look back hopelessly as the wardens carried me away. Now I have power, and I intend to prevent such trauma again from happening again when I can."

"Zach, you can't save everyone, you can't save the whole world. Before Kyiv, we were a whole regiment, now we are only a few. Even Terra and all its technology can't change the world back to the way it was."

"Yeah, Vincent, I know we can't. But for everyone we save, the world is changed forever."

Suddenly, Zach and Vincent heard howling in the distance. An icy feeling of dread went down the two men's spines.

"Vincent? Do you hear that?"

"I do! Fuck! Get to our guns!"

The two rushed over to fetch their weapons but Zach looked back to see glowing yellowish eyes. However, before they could reach their weapons, a giant shape leaped out of the darkness and pounced on Vincent. Zach gaped with pure horror at what looked to be a giant wolf with spines.

"Zach, run! Get your gun!"

Vincent punched at the wolf, scrambling away from the beast. Reaching for his pocket, he brandished his knife. When the wolf leapt at him, he jabbed the knife into the wolf's paw, barely wounding it, yet it still bought him time to escape. Horrified at what was happening, Dimitri got up and ran over to the rest of the team who were still asleep. More of these spiked wolves showed up.

Zach and Vincent reached for their weapons but just as Zach was loading his gun, a wolf pounced at him, knocking him to the ground. Zach then tried to use the butt of his rifle to wallop the wolf in his face. A wolf approached Vincent, but he blazed his gun at the wolf killing it. He then wounded the wolf that was attacking Zach, forcing it to retreat. The howls were getting louder and louder however, as more wolves were approaching. Dimitri ran to the sleeping Alexi and tried shaking him awake.

"Wake up, wake up, monsters are coming! Lots of them!"

Alexi groaned at first until he eventually said, "Eh, what? What is it, kid?"

"Your friends need help! They are being attacked by the monsters!"

Alexi slowly started to get up. His frustration at being woken up vanished when he saw the wolves.

"Wolves. Wolves! WOLVES!" Alexi yelled.

The sound of wolves woke everyone up from their sleep. Eventually, Vincent and Zach managed to retreat to the campfire while the rest of them had just opened their eyes to see the glowing eyes of the wolves starring right back at them.

"Form a circle! Don't let them near!" Michael yelled.

The team scrambled to get their weapons and readied them for the oncoming attack. The wolves began their own encirclement but they seemed to keep their distance from the campfire. Dimitri kept as close to the campfire as possible, hoping that the blazing heat of the campfire would keep the monsters at bay. The spotlights on the guns illuminated small patches and the wolves seemed to stay away from them. A wolf slowly started to approach.

Its saliva drooled as it looked Michael in the eyes. It was most likely the Alpha male of the pack because it was the biggest and toughest of the creatures.

"What is with these wolves? What do they want?" Zach asked curiously.

"Meat," Michael began to explain. "We are meat to them, not often that you find meat in the Badlands. As for spikes well, lessons to be learned from WW3, don't experiment on wolves. If you do, you get these bastards!"

The Alpha approached closer to the campfire, but Dermot fired a shot. It didn't hit the Alpha, but it did cause him to growl and start to back off. They were waiting for the team to come into the darkness. However, the mood suddenly changed and the wolves seemed to be alarmed.

What sounded like a foghorn bellowed through the night. The wolves stopped what they were doing, and the eyes of the Alpha widened. He howled, ordering his pack to retreat from the area. Though a brief sense of relief went through the men, they started to get uneasy as the horn sounded again. Hearing the horn again and seeing the wolves retreat, Dia asked Chang, "Where are they gone?"

"I don't know, but they must be retreating. I suggest we do the same!"

It was then that they all felt the ground shake very rapidly, causing all of them to start shaking. As they readied their weapons, they could see red lights in the pitch-black distance of the night.

"Sir?" Zach said to Michael.

Michael knew all too well what was coming.

"Take the kid, there is a nearby bomb shelter, get him there, right now and just stick with us."

"Eh okay."

The rest of the group gathered together and began to run; they did not want to fight what was coming.

"Wait, guys, what in the name of God is going on?" Zach asked as he grabbed Dimitri.

"The Black Mouth, Zach if you lose that little mutt, our little mission would be for nothing...oh and I've just got to love you...so don't die on me!" Vincent replied.

"I don't intend on doing that anytime soon!"

"Good boy."

The horns sounded again as a giant foot stamped on the ground and emitted steam. Much to his horror, Zach suddenly found himself looking up at the most gigantic machine that he had ever seen in his life. Towering above the men was what looked to be a metallic spider crab, bristling with machine guns that could shred through armour, cameras for eyes, MLRS missile launchers on its back and racks of gas canisters that could be launched from its legs. The abomination was made of titanium; the only way to defeat the monster was to shut it down. Dimitri was too frightened to do anything; he closed his eyes as he clutched onto Zach. The Black Mouth fired canisters into the air. Seeing this, Michael directed the men to fit their gas masks on. Zach helped Dimitri get his mickey mouse gas mask on as the canisters bounced off the ground and then burst, causing a dark greenish mist to seep out. The mist poured through the area like a vengeful spirit and it eventually reached the team.

As ever, the sight of the gas caused Zach to panic and fumble his attempts to fit on his own gas mask. The rest of the team were too focused on getting to the shelter to realise his difficulty. Zach started to run across the snow as he saw the gas come towards him even though he still didn't have his mask on properly.

It was as if Zach was in a nightmare that he couldn't wake up from, for the gas consumed him like some sort of beast. Because of his genetic enhancements, it only caused his eyes to sting and tear up. But this essentially blinded him, and he began coughing violently. Dimitri called to him as loudly as he could and tried to guide him to the shelter, but the boy didn't have the super strength of the men. He clung onto Zach, unwilling to let go of the youth that had saved him. He tried to pull at Zach's gas mask with his tired arms even though they ached with pain. Numb with terror, he knew he was at the mercy of the most terrifying creation made by human hands. Then Chang, Alexi and Dia erupted from the shelter to grab them, dragging both into the shelter.

* * *

Sometime later, Zach opened his eyes to see that he was in some sort of dimly lit building made out of concrete.

"Eh boys...where am I?"

"You're alright boy...we're in the bunker...the gas storm is still going out there so don't leave! Okay?" Dermot replied.

"Yeah...Dermot...what is this place?"

"An old bunker...from World War 3."

Indeed, the team had found themselves in a bunker from the Eastern bloc during the Third World War against the West. It was like a large stone maze with rail networks, arsenals, canteens, sleeping quarters and even a control room.

"Do you think we could find out more about this place, sir?" Zach asked Michael.

"Maybe if the computers are still functional, but we are soldiers, not technicians."

"What do we do now, sir?"

"For now, we stay here for the night! We'll start a fire with one of those barrels!" Michael said to everyone present.

Upon that order, the team continued through the dark corridor, the spotlights on their rifles illuminating the area. Skeletons and mangled bones lay around the place. They salvaged a wooden barrel and some papers scattered on the floor. This enabled them to build a fire to huddle around as they spent the night in the old shelter. Zach and Dimitri sat by themselves.

"Hey, those two still seem to be sitting alone," Dermot said to the group, when he saw the two sitting alone. "How about we let the boys come over to us, shall we?"

"Ah yes."

"Aye, Zach, aren't you going to come over, you know we don't hate you anymore, don't you?" Vincent said.

Zach smiled and stood up.

"Come on, sonny, let's go over." Zach said to Dimitri as he took the kid's hand.

The two came over to sit with the rest of the team.

"So, Zach, how is your little guy doing?" Alexi asked as Zach sat down by the fire.

"As a whole, he's doing quite fine by the looks of it. He doesn't talk much but he's not mine. My aim is to try and return the little kid to his parents. The thing is, I don't even know his name...wait a minute, Alexi... you can speak to him in his own language, can't you?"

Alexi spoke to Dimitri in a gentle voice asking him questions. The two for a while held a dialogue in Russian.

"Zach, his name is Dimitri, that you know..." Alexi said eventually. "And he just told me that he likes you," Alexi continued, "but like any child in this position, he's alone and confused."

"I see, well that is extremely forgiving, given that I basically dragged him into this mess."

"Zach, you weren't the one who dragged him in. The war came to St Petersburg, he's alive because of you."

"Well, yeah, but I am alive because of you guys. Let's face it, I'd probably be finished without you."

The group laughed.

"Yeah, really!" Zach continued. "Guys, do you have any memory of your families?"

The laughing then stopped as they heard that question. They all looked at each other when Zach asked the question.

"The truth is Zach, barely any of us remember our old lives by now, this life in the Legion has been our existence. Our parents are long dead if that is what you were wondering about." Alexi said eventually, breaking the uneasy silence which had developed.

"But don't you guys miss your parents? I mean they did love you?"

"Ah, Zach, we are grown men, of course we miss our parents. We were pressed into service against our will, I was anyway.

Terran Command needed fresh troops at that time, they didn't care much about the emotional consequences of their actions."

Zach felt chilled by that. He thought of his own family at home in New York. It was then a haunting thought came to his mind. These men around him were once new meats like him. They might have had a childhood much like he had and much like Dimitri was currently having. A dreadful thought came to his mind; what if he would become like them someday, harsh, tough with barely any memory of his old life?

"Look on the bright side, Zach, when our family die, they are freed from this miserable life down here. They live in an afterlife. And in the afterlife, there is no war, no crime and no suffering. Consider death a blessing, not a curse!" Dermot said, sensing Zach's anxiety.

"Aw, that's really nice and comforting. I'll do my best to remember that when we are in the heat of battle!" Zach replied.

"Good, because it will make you slightly more comfortable when the time comes for your demise." Dia said.

Eventually, the team got to sleep. They were unaware of the blizzard that was raging outside. When they woke up, their fire was still burning and for the first time they could see something of their surroundings.

CHAPTER 13: THE SHELTER OF REVELATIONS

Observing their surroundings, Chang began a conversation with Michael.

"Sir, do you think that this shelter could have communications arrays?"

"Communications to contact the Tungsten?"

"Yes, or any other flying fortress that is nearby, sir!"

Michael considered for a moment.

"Okay, lads," he said, eventually, "this base could be our chance at reuniting with the rest of the Legion. We are going to search for the control room in the base. That is our best chance at finding radios strong enough to communicate with our flying fortresses. Understood?"

"Understood, sir."

"Good, we're moving out!"

And with that, the men, though they were tired and hungry, went deeper and deeper into the corridors. Even with the spotlights of their rifles shining to illuminate the area, the men felt cold and alone. They came across many more mangled corpses scattered across the floor. They came in all shapes and sizes, but the bones were splintered and scattered with their skulls smashed.

"The savagery? What do you think happened here? The bones look so mangled! Did the machines do this?" Dia said suddenly.

"I don't think so, this bunker doesn't look damaged. One would imagine that it could easily hold out against a machine attack." Chang replied.

"Then what did this to them? Was there a monster?"

"I hate to break it to you, Dia, but I have an ugly feeling that they did this to themselves. We do not need robots for us to degenerate into animals."

"What?? Themselves? Why? How is that practical for

holding out against an enemy?"

"Rational thought does not come easily to people who have run out of food. Imagine staying in this darkness for years, crammed in this place. Surely that has an effect on the mind."

"Are you suggesting they ate each other in this place?" Vincent introjected.

"Don't worry, it's merely speculation on my part." Chang replied.

The men chuckled and Vincent tried to laugh.

"Well boys, this is normally when the slasher comes in the horror movie!" Alexi said.

"As if we are in any way scared, Alexi! One masked slasher with a knife against seven superhuman soldiers with guns, that's not going to go well for the freak!" Michael replied, sarcastically.

"Eh guys, is this a good conversation to have while we are in a place like this?" Zach suggested.

"Are you scared of slashers, Zach?" Alexi asked.

"I'm not, slashers are cheap and boring, a bunch of teenage kids go to an obviously strange house and start to be hacked apart by a masked freak. Where is the fun in that?" Zach said.

"They were made for a generation who never had to deal with losing their mum and dad, Zach, for such a comfortable generation, such things were apparently fun."

The group laughed mockingly as they thought on what Dermot said. Terrans had not much respect for generations who grew up without fearing life or death and who enjoyed violence. Zach however still had the creeps as he looked at the skeletons. In this bleak age of mechanised warfare, there were worse things than slashers to worry about

* * *

Deep in the base they found the central control room. Beneath the cobwebs was a vast room with arrays of seats facing a large computer along with other devices that once were used to project holographic images. It was still pitch black and dead silent.

While the rest of the team were searching for old radios and communication devices, Zach and Dimitri explored the control room till they approached the main computer.

"Well, this place is huge, how many people did they intend on having in this place...hundreds, thousands?" Zach said.

"Thousands."

Dimitri spoke in a tired voice. Zach stopped in shock because this was the first time, he had heard Dimitri speak, at least in English.

"What, you just spoke English? I didn't know you speak English. You are Dimitri, right, that's what Alexi said your name was? How did you learn to speak English?"

"Dimitri, yes, my name is Dimitri. I learned English from my Dad and at school. Everyone has to learn English as a language. That seems to be the way for living in Terra."

"I see. What was his name?"

"His name was Nicholas. Your name is Zach, isn't it?"

"Yes, it is Zach, Zach Harker."

"Zach, are my parents still alive?"

Hearing that question, Zach felt stung. That fear of losing his parents was a fear he knew all too well. But he had seen them dragged onto a dropship, so he answered Dimitri.

"They are, and I think they are waiting for you in Norway, that's where the inhabitants of Saint Petersburg were taken."

"Then I will be able to go home? Won't I?"

"Oh no, if your home was St Petersburg then I'm sorry, but Commander Rufus Thorne basically had your whole city obliterated. The Terran engineers may not be ready to rebuild it yet."

Dimitri looked horrified.

"Why? Why did he do that? Isn't he supposed to be good?"

Zach thought about the question for a long while.

"Yeah, being good doesn't mean being nice, sonny. He didn't want the machines to use your city to produce weapons." Zach began eventually. "When machines take a city, they'd tear it down as well without considering the human cost. Still, I wonder what's going to go through Phil's mind when he discovers what has happened. It's not like he knows that I'm here."

"Who's Phil?"

"My little brother...who didn't nick most of the attention from Mom, probably the main reason we got on so well...but one day, these bullies showed up, they wanted to mutilate Phil. So, I stabbed one of them, and the police came for me!"

"You joined the Legion as punishment...but didn't get a chance to defend yourself in court? Weren't there witnesses?"

"Not for me, the gang told a biased story. According to Terran law, only people present at the crime can stand as witnesses, and Phil was too young to speak at court, so I was charged with murder...and it was either the Legion or the electric chair for me."

Dimitri looked horrified.

"So, you were sentenced because of biased witnesses. That sounds like a story my father would tell about the previous governments who ruled my country."

"Yeah, for all its morality and Christian values, Terran law isn't completely pure of the corruption of the law. I don't think any society is completely free of that kind of evil."

"But surely there is something that can be done about this? Will we ever be free of unjust law?"

Zach wished he could say yes to Dimitri.

"I hate to break it to you sonny, but I don't know. All I know is that I hope we can, and even if it is a fight we can't win, the fight against corruption is a fight worth fighting. But if we are to preserve our society long enough to win that fight, we'll have to win our war against the machines first. I can only pray to God that what has happened to me will not happen to others. Whether my prayer will be answered, I don't know."

CHAPTER 14: THE HARSH TRUTH

Zach knelt down to study a piece of equipment. He was still thinking about the conversation he had just had with Dimitri. He had known full well what would happen to him when he stabbed that bully but still, his little brother was in danger, so he had to act. The law was not God but at least in the Legion he had a life and a chance. However, in some ways, he longed to be a statesman so that someday he could bring an end to some of Terra's cruel practices in the same way Lincoln sought to bring an end to slavery. He looked at Dimitri who had knelt down beside him. It was only now that Zach really realised how much Dimitri reminded him of what he was once like. A young boy lost and confused in the middle of a war.

After a little while, Dimitri saw a button on the side of the machine. Curious, he pressed it and jumped back in shock as a holographic image rose in front of them. The hologram showed various violent images depicting massive war machines, entrenchments, atomic testing, robots and other graphic images of war. The sounds of warfare and dramatic speeches emitted from the image, ringing through the ears of both Zach and Dimitri.

"Okay...what is all this about? World War Three?" Zach asked in amazement.

The rest of the squad came over to watch the film playing in front of them. They shook their heads in confusion. Then suddenly an Asiatic man in a white coat showed up in the hologram and said in a very sad and horrified voice:

To anyone who reads this message...this is the worst mistake I have ever made! By employing these robotic abominations for our hastily scrambled alliance, I thought I was reducing the chance of seeing my people get butchered by the meat grinder of war.
I did what no other scientist did, I gave my creation, the Black Mouth, intelligence. I gave it a brain and forged it out of titanium! I created

a monster to defend my people from the American war machine! But I never gave it a conscience or a heart! That was my mistake. The Black Mouth felt only one emotion! Rage, rage towards mankind! It transmitted its anger to all machines! And the machines turned on humanity. Russia, China, America, the whole world has fallen to the iron fist of the machines. Only Europe stands, Europe and its Legions stand. For all those around the world still alive, stand, stand as humans! Fight on! Don't let the Black Mouth consume you!

Everyone was speechless. Even Chang, who was usually as stoic as a rock, shed a tear as he suddenly remembered hearing tales of his great grandparents getting to a ship in order to escape westward to Europe. Zach remembered hearing about all this in school, and that the Legion held the line to stop the world from being consumed. He was worried about the idea that the Black Mouth had travelled the world. What about those undiscovered tribes who had no notion of science? To them, it would have been some sort of devil. He hoped it never reached them.

"So, the Black Mouth was created not to attack but to protect?" Zach asked Michael.

"Yes, that is true! The Black Mouth was the Sino-Russian alliance's last hope in beating back America's invasion. It was designed to hack enemy robots and turn them against their commanders. But the Black Mouth had deeper plans by the looks of it. Once it developed its own agenda, there was very little we could do to stop it."

"But why? They deployed so many other assets. Why did they create something so dangerous?"

Zach felt like he actually didn't want to know the answer, but he asked anyway. And it was Alexi who answered Zach.

"Do you not see, kid? For the same reason your America created the atomic bomb, for the same reason, the British sent the tank hurtling over No Man's Land and for the same reason that we were transformed into metahumans by the Terran government. They wanted to win a war that had gone on too long! Nothing creates horror like desperation!"

Zach went silent upon hearing these words. All of the team

went silent. It was unsettling to consider that the same instinct that created the Legion was also the same instinct that created the Black Mouth and its monstrosities. That instinct was survival. Suddenly Dia spoke, trying to raise the team's morale.

"Look on the bright side! Think of our modern country, Terra! This threat of the Black Mouth, it unified us Europeans, Americans, Polynesians, Asians and Africans in a way that no progressive politician could ever hope to. We are now all men, regardless of our skin, our Gods and of who we choose to love. We may all have our different traditions and practices but now we have each other. As sad as the war is, let's not forget that."

"Well, that is a nice morale boost, Dia! Still, we have a job to do and we need to get that kid back to his parents! What the hell do we do now?" Vincent said.

Before anyone could answer, the horns of the Black Mouth sounded very close. Without warning, its massive foot tore through the bunker stamping not far from where the group was.

"Does that answer your question, Vincent?" Alexi said.

"Yeah...I suggest we get the fuck out of here!!"

* * *

The team rushed out of the bunker, and onto the ice. Around them the heat of the explosions of the rounds being shot at them were causing the ice to crack. Michael gathered the group together and made them stop. The ice cracked up all around them, splitting apart violently. Water spewed out of the cracks as the ice split apart.

Next thing they spotted a flying fortress, the *Valiant*, approaching the Black Mouth and opening fire on it. But it was no match for the monster, its rounds of ammunition simply bounced off its body. In return, the Black Mouth fired missiles at it, severely damaging the vessel, forcing it to retreat. One of its dropships that it had released to patrol quickly followed, but not before its co-pilot had noticed the group huddled together on a piece of ice.

"Christ, I think I might have seen Alpha Squad down there!"

He said to the pilot.

"What? We can't go back for them...not while that abomination is still there, pull out!!"

Zach shielded Dimitri from the debris and the water as the ice floe that they were on floated aimlessly in the North Sea. He felt a sense of hopelessness as he looked up. That flying fortress was a chance at getting home but now it was crippled. The flying fortress slowly limped back to an aerodrome as its crew struggled to extinguish the raging fires that had broken out on the vessel.

* * *

Meanwhile, up at the battered bridge of the vessel, amidst the howling of the alarms, an officer was speaking to his captain.

"Captain! Our vessel is badly damaged, should we report to the *Tungsten* on Alpha Squad's disappearance?"

The captain looked around him as sparks emitted from the damaged devices on board. Crewmen got to work extinguishing fires on the bridge while alarms rang throughout the vessel.

"We turn back to the nearest aerodrome! Inform Commander Thorne of the situation! The disappearance of Alpha Squad will not rest lightly on the hearts of the Terran public!"

"Understood, sir!"

* * *

Back at the Tungsten, things were going as usual. Jethro was observing the holographic map when an officer came bursting into the control room. Jethro turned to see the panicked officer frantically salute him.

"Report! What has happened?" Jethro said to the officer who approached him.

"Sir, we got news from the *Valiant*!"

"Has Alpha Squad been located?"

"Yes, sir, Alpha Squad might have been located but..."

"What?"

"The Black Mouth, sir! The Black Mouth was encountered, and it crippled the *Valiant!*"

The sound of this sent ice down Jethro's spine. The Black Mouth was a machine that was practically indestructible. Even the *Kirov*, the strongest flying fortress, would be incapable of denting the Black Mouth.

"Still no sign of Alpha Squad, Colonel?" Rufus said to Jethro when he appeared

"Sir...we've checked everywhere...their most likely area of disappearance is the North Sea. Rumours have it that the *Valiant* discovered the squad but it was forced to retreat due to the Black Mouth crippling it! Commander Thorne, we need more resources to continue..."

But Rufus had had enough. The crippling of the *Valiant* had killed countless personnel and Legionnaires. He was not going to risk the whole Legion for the sake of one small team. He had an offensive to coordinate.

"Cancel the search! This pathetic distraction has gone on long enough, we need to get back to Saint Petersburg!"

Shocked by this, Jethro responded angrily.

"Commander Thorne!! You can't just do that! That squad is one of our best...you need to continue the s..."

"I have a whole race to defend Colonel! That is enough pressure to swallow!"

Jethro was speechless with horror at Throne's attitude. For him, the capacity to display such apathy for individual soldiers, especially ones who had served with the Legion for so long, was unimaginable. He turned and left the bridge. An officer followed him.

"Later when the situation is less intensive, we will seek permission to continue the search." Jethro said to the officer.

The officer tapped the visor of his cap.

"Understood, sir."

✱ ✱ ✱

Meanwhile back in New York, night had settled over the sky and the city had lit up its lights. The Statue of Liberty's torch was brightly lit up and its glow could be seen for miles. Having worked yet another night shift, Valentine had come home exhausted where she found Phil watching the news. The main headline was about the war, much progress had been gained. On the news were scenes of flying fortresses performing bombardment, giant tanks hurtling through industrial facilities as well as Legionnaires engaged in actions. As these scenes played out, a news commentator was making an announcement in a very smooth and refined tone as he said triumphantly:

This evening, the scenario has re-stabilized once again thanks to the efforts of our brave Legionnaires!! Our defeat at St Petersburg did not hinder their noble efforts as they recovered their initiative and have successfully commenced the reclaiming of lost territory. They are now counterattacking the machines as they besiege the machine-held city of St Petersburg! The fronts of today's warfare are fickle, and we will keep you informed with more updates!

Concerned about the effect on Phil of news of that kind, she sat down on the couch beside him.

"Phil, come on, what are you doing watching news like this?"

"Just wanted to find out about Zach, Mom."

"I doubt he'd be on the news, Phil. Come on, let's go to bed."

"But Mom, Zach..."

"Philip! You're too young for this kind of violence."

"But I've watched action movies! Especially those from the eighties and the Classic Bonds!"

Valentine breathed deeply.

"Real life warfare is nothing like action movies! Don't watch war news with the expectation that it would be like an Indiana Jones fist fight. If that was the case, then there would be something seriously wrong with the Terran news system. Come on, Phil, you'll need that sleep for tomorrow!"

She was just about to switch off when suddenly she heard the news commentor continue:

And a further news item tonight is about the possible fate of Team Orca, as they are familiarly called. Since the St Petersburg disaster, the Alpha Squad has been lost for several days, and they were last seen in the Northern Badlands where they are believed to have gone missing. This is a massive blow since they were one of the best teams of Legionnaires. If they have indeed died, then the St Petersburg disaster will prove to be a much greater setback to the army then anticipated...We will have more updates for you as the week goes on. Ladies and Gentlemen, goodnight.

Speechless, Valentine turned off the TV. She tried to reassure herself that they weren't dead. After all, Legionnaires didn't die easily. It took a lot to kill a Legionnaire. Especially a squad of very experienced Legionnaires like the Alpha Squad.

"Mom? Does that mean Zach is...?" Phil asked her suddenly.

Before he could finish his question, Valentine put her arms around him and hugged him tightly.

"No, come on, chill down, Zach is not dead...they didn't confirm them as dead, okay Phil? It's alright...Zach's gonna be okay."

* * *

It was a stormy night in the coastal city of Tromso, Norway where the St Petersburg refugees had been settled in a big refugee camp. It soon developed into a vast locale surrounded by fences and outposts. Within the camp were a plethora of large tents equipped with proper lighting, heating, sanitation facilities and beds so as to make their current misery slightly more bearable till the day that Saint Petersburg could be repopulated. The Home Guard kept a good watch out for machines. Dressed in long coats with assault rifles slung over their shoulders, armed guards with furry circular caps known as ushankas kept order in the camp. People, draped in winter clothes or furs, queued up for their rations.

Anya was in one of those queues, but her husband wasn't with her because he was too broken over the loss of Dimitri. A guard yelled at the people to keep in line, but he mostly spoke in Norwegian, which Anya barely understood. It was only when they spoke English that she somewhat understood them. Behind her, she heard a voice ask

"Is it true? Have Alpha Squad perished?"

Anya turned around to see who had spoken. It was an old man with a crusty old beard.

"I don't know, that's what's being spread on the news. Did you know any of its members?"

"My friend had a son named Alexi, that boy became part of the squad."

"I'm sorry."

"You are not to blame...God I respect those boys."

Later after getting a ration of food, Anya hurried back to their tent where she found Nicholas, sitting staring into space. She sat down to try and coax him to eat something but he shook his head and looked at her with very pained eyes. She put her arm around his shoulders as if trying to communicate to him her belief that Dimitri might still be alive out there. The two then embraced.

CHAPTER 15: PRESUMED DEAD

Across the ocean and back somewhere over the skies in Eastern Europe in the Tungsten, the tape recorder played a classical piece in the background as Rufus sat in the sitting room reserved for officers. The sitting room had a very ornate interior and had a set of armchairs, a cupboard, several tables and even a pool table. Groups of officers, dressed in their smart green uniforms, relaxed by having drinks, smoking cigarettes and playing card games such as poker. A team of officers were playing a game of pool among themselves.

Decorating the sitting room were statues, mainly of gods, goddesses and archangels. There was even a painting of Saint George slaying the dragon. For Terrans, such an image was a common metaphor for humanity's struggle against the chaotic world around them, especially at this time when they waged war with the machines, monsters of their own creation. At the pool table, the officers spoke among themselves.

"Did you hear about Rufus Thorne today? He just ordered a cancellation of the search for Alpha Squad." One said but his comrade responded apathetically.

"I know but who cares? It's a war! Casualties happen, we can't always be squandering resources based on moral virtue."

"Moral virtue? These lads are one of our best squads, a squad as qualified as Alpha Squad is not as easy to come by. Such men are not cheap. They win our wars!"

"So what? It's sad but that is war. We can't be worrying about a bunch of boots!"

"Boots? Is that what you call the men on the ground? Just as well that they can't hear you. With that kind of attitude, you'd probably end up having to face a mutiny! That's the last thing we need during a scenario in which we fight for our own bitter survival!"

Rufus finished his cigarette then threw the butt in the

bin. At the edge of the sitting room, there was a window which overlooked the night sky.

Looking from the window, it was possible to see the encamped Terran armies who were entrenched for the night. The door opened as Jethro walked into the sitting room. Seeing Rufus, he came over and sat on the opposite armchair.

"Commander Thorne...we badly need to have a serious talk." Jethro said sternly, as Thorne met his eyes.

Rufus looked at him wearily before replying.

"This is about Alpha Squad, isn't it, Colonel Jethro?"

"You are very skilled at reading my mind, Commander Thorne. That is exactly why I came here!"

All the officers stopped what they were doing, and all eyes turned to look at Rufus Thorne. Rufus sighed. Even as they were starting to reclaim the Eurasian continent from the machines, the fate of Alpha Squad still lay heavy on Thorne. Without looking around him, he could feel that all the officers were looking at him. He however wanted to have the conversation with Jethro in private.

"Gentlemen you must pardon this request, but Colonel Jethro and I need to have a word in private... please leave us!" He announced to the men.

The other officers left the room, muttering and whispering among each other as they went. Rufus took out two wine glasses, and a bottle of red wine. As he slowly poured the bright red wine into the glasses, he spoke in a solemn voice.

"The disappearance and possible death of Michael and his men weighs heavily on you, doesn't it?"

"We can't leave them out there!"

Rufus looked at Jethro in the eye.

"What of it? We have a war to win! We have to maintain the offensive across Eurasia in order to win this dreadful war."

Jethro was shocked at Throne's attitude.

"What do you mean when you say...what of it??" He said angrily. "Don't you have any concern for legionnaires...that squad is one of the last of the conscripted legionnaires...the very boys we took from their parents to make them into killing machines that could easily match the machines in battle! I was one of them, one among a thousand and I oversaw the training of a thousand more...it is their courage that has ensured that humanity exists today...and that you have a uniform laden with medals and badges! That is why I do everything that ensures the survival of as many legionnaires as I can...and since you have all the resources that the military has to offer...I need your help!!"

Rufus was silent as he drank more wine. He spoke with a heavy voice.

"Colonel Jethro...I am very aware that the mass conscription of boys from 13 onwards makes me and my fellow officers not so different from the abominations that we decimate on a regular basis...but it is dumb to theorise that that decision doesn't weigh on any politician..."

"Commander, what are you getting at?"

"If we hadn't been in such a desperate position, we would never have done such a tragic act...take a look outside."

Standing up, Rufus and Jethro went over to look outside the window at all the other flying fortresses flying over the enormous encampments below them. The sound of the 'Lacrimosa', a lament by Mozart, played on the radio.

"Colonel,", Rufus began, sternly, "if any of those cities or flying fortresses get destroyed, the responsibility is on my shoulders...I've got way too much to deal with and keep preserved in order to waste my time with micro-management. The government of Terra expects me to do my duty and I do it every day! But not without a price! The price of blood and death. Civilisation is built and preserved not on money or capital, or wishes granted by fairy godmothers, no, it is built on the blood of men. From the labourers carving out our great structures to the boys, barely men, charging into battle at the sound of the bugle. And now, Terra, much like all other countries and empires that came before it, must sacrifice the blood of its men to preserve its existence. For all the modernity we have accomplished, for all the technology we have developed, for all the social progress that society has made, for all the choices our modern democracy claims to have given to us, we still must kill other beings to preserve our existence. That is the harsh truth of civilisation, Colonel."

Jethro was silent as he digested what Thorne had said.

"So, you are going to..." He replied, eventually.

"Colonel Jethro," Rufus interrupted, "the *Tungsten* is preparing to do a patrol up into the North Sea, not too far from where we last heard of Michael and his men. We will then be stopping off at Tromso, a key city in Norway's far north to bolster our supplies!"

"Wait, does that mean we are actually going after them? You're not as heartless as I thought you were."

"Well, Colonel, you too have considerable power...I give you the freedom to perform the micromanagement that I am incapable of carrying out! Do not squander such power pointlessly!"

"Thank you, sir!"

Jethro saluted and left the room, leaving Rufus alone, still gazing on the scene below. The horrors of the battlefield were alien and distant to Rufus as he observed the progress of the war on a holographic screen from the safety and security of his flying fortress. However, that didn't mean he wasn't as badly affected by it mentally as the troops were. At least when they lost, they died and went to the afterlife but Rufus, when he lost a battle, had to live with the guilt of defeat. He had to live with the knowledge that one day he might be forced to look into the eyes of the parents whose sons he sent to their death whenever an order was issued. For all the suffering his actions caused, he felt the full weight of his responsibilities. Rufus was not the heartless bourgeois general that a thinker like Marx would claim he was.

* * *

The offensive was to continue the following day regardless of the news about Alpha Squad. The sooner the Legion was able to punch through the Urals, the sooner they would be able to cripple the machine's industrial heartland in the plains of Eurasia. If that could be achieved, the machines would be knocked out of the war. Down below, encampments were made by troops of Legionnaires who settled down around fires to keep themselves warm from the cold wind of the Tundra landscape that surrounded their camp. Sentries kept watch so that the men would be able to ward off any surprise attack launched by the machines. Vehicles were parked near encampments and they were at the ready in case of an attack. Entrenchments were already being dug to help fortify the position.

* * *

Adrift on the ice floe, Zach dreamed a lot about his mother and brother. Phil barely got to know his father since it was only a few years after his birth that their father had died in the gas attack, but Zach had quite a deep relationship with his parents, especially his father.

Like every single soldier that ever lived, it was when he was on the verge of possible death that he missed his family the most. He lay there, coming to realise how much he missed looking at the blue eyes and curly reddish-brown hair of his mother that often reached loosely to her shoulders. By the time he was eighteen, he was really taking the place of his father, as he was already starting to become taller and broader than his mother and he looked out for Phil a lot. In his sleep, Zach dreamed of the time when Valentine told Phil the story of the Salmon of Knowledge and how Fíonn managed to blend in with the Fianna, even becoming their most respected leader.

At the time it just felt like another story but that night was the night before he murdered the bully. His days as a civilian were gone, and, although he still only a new meat, his body had become broader and fitter. Due to the strength gained from both genetic enhancement and intense training, Zach was probably strong enough to lift his mother in his arms. He wasn't even through his first mission, but already the skimpy, terrified boy who feared ghosts and banshees, the boy once called Zach, was dead. The intense physical exercise, genetic modifications and the first day in combat had killed him. In his place, lying down on the iceberg with Dimitri firmly in his arms, was the man named Zach Harker.

He was woken up by some sort of high-pitched noise coming from the water. Surfacing from the icy water was a whale. The huge creature came up briefly before it plunged back down, swishing its tail up into the air before diving back into the water. Surprised, Zach got up and looked over into the water to see the whale swimming alongside its calf. The sound of the whale's noise and its sheer size made Zach feel tiny in comparison as he gazed down at the creature, seeing it plunge deep into the water and disappear into the depths below. Woken up, Dimitri noticed the whale as it disappeared. He gasped in awe as he had never seen a whale so close before. He was fascinated by what he had seen.

"Wow, that was big, wasn't it?" Dimitri said to Zach.

"I know right...I just felt so...small in its wake!"

"Why is that?"

"I don't know...it's just we're on such a small ice piece...and I just look down there and think...just think...we've made massive strides in technology, we've developed replication, AI, nuclear fusion, space travel, heavily developed colonies that probably don't even know about this war, massive craft that can go far into space, hydrogen fuel, yet, despite all that, we still know barely anything about the ocean's depths. It's strange, a whole new world. The thing is that when you hear a lion roar or a chimpanzee screech that's all you hear, a roar, just a noise, but when you hear a whale sing, it's like you're hearing a language being spoken, emotions being conveyed. It's something that we can't just rationalize."

"Rationalize? What do you mean by rationalize?"

"Yeah, rationalize, the desire of humanity to just force everything to make sense. You know, rip out all of the mystery of the world and put it into categories, tell children how to think about it. Make it fit some sort of abstract worldview, a worldview that tells us that there is no such thing as good and evil, that God, faeries, Jesus and Mother Earth are little more than childish superstitions that apparently must be grown out of. By the logic of reason, you should have died. In the eyes of reason, you are a drag to the team."

Tears welled up in Dimitri's eyes.

"Then why did you come for me, Zach? Why did you guys risk your lives to bring me back to my mum?"

Wiping the tears off Dimitri's cheeks, Zach spoke to him firmly.

"Listen, kid, there is one thing that reason cannot explain away, and that is *emotion*. Emotion is a part of us, it is the part that causes us to care for each other, that part that bonds us, the essence that links us to our fellow human beings. Mark me, Dimitri, emotion was what brought me to rescue you, my heart is what told me to save you. It sounds childish to say this in a world as muddled and as complex as ours but listen to your heart sonny. So long as empathy remains unconquered, the world is capable of good."

"Does your brother look like me?" Dimitri asked with a smile.

"You have the same body structure yes, the blue eyes yes, but he has brown hair ...aside from that though you share a lot of similarities."

"Do you miss your mum, Zach? Stories say that Legionnaires have no feelings, That's what grown-ups say about guys like you. Yet you lot have proved me wrong."

Zach looked unsure as to how to answer that question without triggering an emotional outburst.

"Why would you think I wouldn't? You know Dimitri, a lot of people, when they think of soldiers, they just think of a bunch of hunky beasts with machine guns that just blow stuff up and yell their heads off...hell, that was the image I got of them thanks to the games I played. Then when I got pushed into the Legion, I realised that there was a lot more to a soldier than a smart haircut and uniform...war is a tragic experience for anyone but there is one glory about it...is that when you're back-to-back with someone in the face of a monster...you just care that he could save your life. That's something I never experienced in school. I thought I'd leave life hating the squad I'm with but now I suddenly realise there's more to them than just a bunch of brutes. That they do have emotions. And they may be crass to each other in the bunk room but not in the Badlands."

Zach and Dimitri hugged each other.

"Do you think I'll ever have a brother?" Dimitri asked.

"I don't know...most boys probably dread the day that they'll have a little brother...I was worried about Phil's birth...but then when he was born...he wasn't so bad."

CHAPTER 16: THE SQUID

The following morning, Michael saw something very big emerging from the water in the distance. Much to his relief, it was an "archer class" submarine. These enormous underwater vessels were another marvel of advanced engineering. They could delve much deeper than the submarines of the twenty first century as they had fusion cores and pressure control devices that allowed them to withstand enormous amounts of pressure. Its giant hull had a curved cylindrical shape like most submarines, and it had a conning tower at the stern of the vessel in which the bridge was located. Two large triangular wings extended from either side of the submarine's hull. Decorating the hull were turrets that launched torpedoes. Notably, the vessel had the insignia from the underwater nation of Atlantica, an ally of Terra during the war.

Two fins extended from either side of the front of the submarine which also contained the vessel's torpedo tubes. Each torpedo had a tracking device that allowed them to fire off in any direction. It also had the ability to launch smaller fighter submarines and it could deploy squads of aquanaut marines. The sight of the submarine in the distance gave Michael hope, so he woke up the team, ordering them to make as much noise as possible in order to attract attention.

Eventually, in desperation, Michael brandished his flare gun and fired a flare. The flare soared up into the air, but before it could reach a significant enough height for the captains of the submarine to see it, it fizzled out. A rumble could be heard in the distance after which the submarine submerged out of sight, much to the whole team's despair.

"Well, it seems to be too busy to notice us...can we contact it, Captain?" Dermot asked Michael.

"No...our side radios don't have enough signal...they're probably useless because of the fact that they are soaked. Come on boys, we need to find some way to attract any Terran or Atlantican unit in order to get ourselves picked up!"

Vincent, peering through binoculars, noticed an abandoned uplink on the cliffs.

"Boys!! There's an uplink up at the cliffs, I suggest we use it!"

"Yeah, good idea, Vincent...only that our ice floe drifts randomly...it doesn't have an engine!" Alexi snapped back, irritated.

"Then we'll give it an engine!" Michael introjected.

"Give it an engine, sir? What do you mean by that?"

"I mean manpower, Alexi, before the steam engine or sails came into existence it was physical strength that drove our craft! Vincent, Dermot and Alexi, come with me! All of you, strip!"

"Strip? You mean take off all our clothes, sir?" Dermot said.

Michael took off his armour and proceeded to strip off his dark brown uniform underneath. He answered with exaggerated politeness

"Well, you don't want to tread around in a wet uniform do you, Dermot?"

"Of course not, that would just slow us down, sir."

"Then do as I say...strip! That's an order!"

The men took off their uniforms. They only kept their underpants on, which in Terran society were often like swimming shorts. Chang, Dia and Zach stayed with Dimitri on the ice floe, ready to keep the other four covered. Michael, Dermot, Alexi and Vincent all used their strength and swimming skills to push the iceberg towards the coast.

* * *

The waves were completely against them as they pushed the ice floe towards the shore, using only their sheer physical strength. Zach, forgetting to brace against the movement of the waves, got knocked off the ice floe and plummeted into the water. Horrified, Dimitri rushed towards the edge of the ice in the hope of reaching out to Zach but was restrained by Chang in order to stop the boy from making a suicidal attempt at heroism. Seeing Zach begin to disappear under the waves, Chang felt a surge of dread as he scrambled over across the ice piece. He tried to grab Zach's hand to haul him back onto the ice piece while at the same time trying to hold onto Dimitri. However, the waves proved to be stronger than Chang. The freezing water weakened Zach, causing him to let go and disappear beneath the waves.

"Zach?? Zach!!! Captain.... Zach's gone overboard!" Chang yelled.

The sound of the harsh stormy weather and the crashing waves of the North Sea drowned out Chang's voice. It was impossible for Michael to hear him.

Zach woke up in the water, desperately struggling to recover. Although confused, his survival instinct kicked in and he started to swim up towards the surface. It was then he saw the commotion above. Suddenly, he looked down and found that he had company. A colossal squid approached him with its hooked tentacles outstretched. Panicking at the sight of this monster he started to struggle as the tentacles began to engulf him. He clung onto his knife and began to hack away at the tentacles, but they grabbed onto him, and began to drag him down deeper into the depths; depths that would probably have crushed an ordinary human being, but not a Legionnaire.

Despite this, the situation for Zach seemed hopeless as he was firmly enclosed in the tight grip of the squid. The hooks on the tentacles were starting to pierce through Zach's skin and his blood poured into the water.

He continued his struggle, but the squid was dragging him deeper and deeper, increasing the pressure on his lungs. Bubbles emitted from his mouth.

At that moment, it seemed that he was damned to die in the depths, his body never to be recovered. Though his body was stronger than that of normal humans, its continued resistance led to what seemed to be a slower and more agonising death. But Zach refused to give up. In an attempt to boost his morale, he thought of his home and childhood as he stubbornly continued to wrestle his way out of the hooked tentacles even as they continued to tear into his limbs.

＊ ＊ ＊

At the same time, up on the surface, the ice floe had reached a shoreline, pushed there by the superhuman strength of the Legionnaires. The moment Chang saw Michael come ashore he yelled

"Captain!! Captain!!!"

"What?"

"Zach's gone down underwater, taken by a wave. I...I tried to rescue him and tried to warn you..."

"What?? What do you mean Zach went underwater?? How did you let that happen??"

"But sir! Forgive me but I was trying to keep the little boy alive at the same time! The child wouldn't have stood a chance in the waters of the North Sea! Zach could be still out there!"

Michael didn't have time for an argument with Chang, so he turned to Dermot and Vincent.

"Dermot! Vincent! Get back into the water and fetch Zach! Even if he's dead, you bring back his corpse! Nobody's leaving the area until we find him!"

Dermot and Vincent dived back into the water. They were armed with knives so that they could defend themselves against any monsters encountered in the depths. As he watched them, Dimitri sat there shivering. He felt a sense of guilt at what happened to Zach. If Zach hadn't gone off to retrieve him, this whole disaster wouldn't have occurred.

Michael looked down at the boy for a brief moment. The boy felt nervous but Michael merely patted Dimitri on the head as if to reassure him that things would be alright. Seeing the boy continue to huddle as he did, Alexi helped Dimitri take off his wet clothes and draped his coat over him to help keep the boy warm.

Michael looked at Chang, who was peering out into the North Sea.

"The mess we get into when we act selflessly, eh Chang?" Michael began. "But one good thing about the boy is that he caused

Zach to man up and display utility."

* * *

Plunging into the freezing waters, Dermot and Vincent swam down into the depths where the deadly struggle was taking place. Zach was beginning to lose consciousness as Dermot plucked Zach from the tentacles while Vincent hacked at the squid. Blood swirled around them as they dragged Zach back to the surface and shoved him onto the coastline where the others were waiting. The two laid Zach down on the beach. Dimitri came over only to see that Zach's body was patterned with vicious wounds that were bleeding profusely. Alexi held the boy back.

"Wait, don't go too close Dimitri, he looks badly wounded."

"Is he alright?" Michael asked Dermot as he rushed over.

"I think he's alive sir...but I don't know! Shit, my CPR skills better pay off...Vincent hold him in place!"

Vincent and Michael held onto him while Dermot did chest compressions. Several long minutes passed till Zach violently coughed up water and blood as he came round, opening his eyes wide.

"What the...? What just happened? What the fuck was that...that...thing?" A confused and shocked Zach said eventually.

"You're with us, Zach. It was a squid...yeah, we plucked you from that beast... it is probably dead now. We made it bleed so that some creature might come and gobble it up!" Vincent replied.

As he sat up, Zach gasped. He could barely move because he was in such agony.

"That squid?" He asked eventually, "Was that modified too?"

"Possibly, there were a lot of freak experiments done during the Third World War...but don't worry, mate! You're safe with us for the time being!"

Zach panted but then started to laugh, shocked and relieved that he narrowly escaped death. The rest of the team were beginning to laugh as well. Coming over, Alexi patted Zach on the shoulder.

"Well, little Harker, scared or surprised? A lot of creeps go swimming in these waters!"

"Scared? Of course, I was scared, how else do you react when you're being dragged down by an enormous squid. Muscles only do so much when you are trapped in such a creature's tentacles, buddy!"

"That's why you always bring mates throughout your life. As annoying as you might find them in a civilised society, you'll never know when you need them." Alexi responded.

"Yeah, well if there is one thing that I can be sure about is that I'm learning that lesson pretty quickly, guys."

The group all shared a burst of laughter as they huddled around each other.

Sometime later, Zach sat on a rucksack, while Dermot fetched bandages to wrap around the vicious wounds that were visible on Zach's body.

The salt from the water made Zach's body sting even more. He was drained of energy from his experience. Dermot stitched up Zach's wounds and covered them with bandages.

"God, thanks guys, I would've been a goner if it weren't for you. Why don't sick bastards like that go extinct...it's always the nice beasts that go extinct, isn't it? Never the bugs!" Zach said to Dermot.

"I hate to break it to you Zach, but you don't survive the natural world by being cute! You survive by being strong. And if you are a mammal, you survive by being caring to your fellow kind. Invertebrates are ugly but they are strong and enduring. It's scary but it's life!"

Zach smiled strangely. He grasped his flask, and he drank from it. As he thought back on what had happened to him, he felt numb and dumbstruck. One moment, it seemed that he was finally doomed to die in the depths, his body lost to any of those who loved him or cared for him. The next thing, he was safely on the shore with his mates.

* * *

Meanwhile, up on the cliff head, Michael was on the lookout for vessels from the Terran fleet. He hoped that they could somehow attract the attention of a ship. If they could, they could be rescued, and they could make it back to be with the rest of the army. However, that submarine they had seen earlier had long gone.

"Any luck, Captain? Are you sure that we couldn't contact them with our radios? Do we still have flares?" Dia said as he approached Michael.

"No, even from the cliff our signals would be too weak, the flare wasn't much good in attracting them either. If we're going to receive any assistance or rescue, then what we need is to get a bigger signal…"

"So, what are our orders, sir?"

Peering ahead through his binoculars, Michael could see the uplink from where he was. This gave him hope because it looked bigger than it was before.

"Same as before, we head to the uplink! Come on, we need to head out!" He said to Dia.

* * *

Back at the camp, the group were gathering their equipment together and cleaning their weapons. Zach was back in his uniform, feeling very sore from the rudimentary surgery Dermot had administered.

"You okay, little buddy?" He said to Dimitri.

Looking at the boy's face, Zach could tell that he was exhausted. The area around Dimitri's eyes looked as red as a lobster. The boy was an unaltered human after all, it was a massive achievement that the kid was able to survive for so long.

"Do you know when I'll find my parents again?"

Zach felt uncomfortable responding to the question. He had no idea of where the group even was. All he knew was that they were near the North Sea, and that Dimitri's parents had been evacuated to the Norwegian coast, where? He didn't know. He wasn't sure how to answer Dimitri's question because he didn't know when they would reach Norway, or even if they would be able to reach Norway alive at this point. That being said, he could see how anxious the boy looked and it felt wrong not to answer.

"I wish I knew kid, but the ugly truth is that I don't know when I'll find your folks."

"What do you mean you don't know? Zach?"

"Well kid, I have news for you! I don't know everything. We're as lost as you are here! I... I... I..."

Zach looked down at his hand only to notice that he had lost his watch along the way during the fiasco on the iceberg.

"I don't know even know what time it is. We've lost track of the days." He said eventually, after a pause.

"There is a chance for everything, isn't there?" Dimitri said, leaning against him.

"I guess there is, kid...I hope there is."

Michael and Dia returned to the camp. Seeing Michael, all the others stood up expectantly. Michael approached Chang.

"Chang, are the boys ready? We're closer to the uplink! It's within walking distance! It's time we move!"

Chang's eyes widened. He knew that the whole team was worn out as a result of being endlessly on the run. For most of their journey, their rest was robbed, first by the wolves and then by the Black Mouth. Even the brief sleep that they had managed to achieve on the ice piece was then burnt out from heaving the ice piece to shore.

"Sir, the men are exhausted! We must rest now. Our attempts at sleep have constantly been disrupted, we need time to recuperate and re organise!" Chang replied.

"Chang! We're on the beach! The Black Mouth will have sent signals to its machines to inform them that we are in the Badlands. If they find us on a beach, they'll pin us down with suppressive fire. At least the uplink will have some level of fortification needed to defend ourselves! You hear me?"

Chang stared dumbly because he was not going to continue arguing with his superior officer. Realizing this, Michael made an announcement to the team.

"Gentlemen! I finally have some good news for you all! There is an uplink that is within walking distance from the beach! At that uplink, there's a chance that we will be able to contact the *Tungsten*! In doing so, we will be able to get help and a much-needed lift home!"

Upon hearing Michael's words, all the team smiled grimly. Though exhausted, they were more than glad to know that the nightmare they had gone through during their foray into the Badlands was finally coming to an end. Zach in particular felt a sense of both disbelief and relief at the same time. Dimitri finally allowed himself to smile because he knew that with a lift home, he would finally be safe with his parents. Neither Zach nor Dimitri cheered like the rest, but they did smile.

***

Sometime later, the team suited up and embarked on their journey to the uplink. Zach's wounds were starting to improve but even though they were less painful, he still walked at a slower pace than the rest of the group. Dimitri started to notice how awkwardly and slowly Zach was moving.

"You alright?" He asked Zach.

"Yeah, I'm surprisingly healthy for someone attacked by a mutant squid."

"My mother never let me swim in the sea for that reason. I heard tales of monsters dwelling in the deep. Do you think you'll be fine?"

"Sonny, there's a simple quote from Friedrich Nietzsche that says, 'that which does not kill us, makes us stronger!'"
"Who's he?"

"A philosopher. Don't worry kid, you'll know many philosophers before you grow up."

The group continued their journey, their legs straining under the effort to heave their hefty bodies up to the uplink. Zach clung onto Dimitri's arm to help him. Eventually they reached the uplink and entered it. The uplink itself was old and abandoned. Much like the shelter they had been in earlier, it was another relic from the Third World War. As a result, it was covered with cobwebs and dust. Despite this, it could be a functional uplink and still capable of sending a large signal. After exploring the place, the team approached the central control panel.

Chang inspected it as the others shined torches to illuminate what he was doing. As he examined the control panel and he fiddled with the switches, Michael spoke to him.

"Do you think this device is functional, Chang?"

"I don't know, it might be, Captain. If it makes you comfortable, these analogue devices from the 20th and 21st centuries are much more endurant than even our most sophisticated digital technologies to the effects of time..."

"But you think that you can get it to work??"

"I'll try, Zach, you and Dimitri were able to get the hologram in the previous shelter up and running, could you two give me a hand?"

Zach and Dimitri came up to the control panel to scan the controls. Zach shined a torch close to the controls, illuminating a big red button. Seeing it lit up, Dimitri pointed to it.

"That's it, that must be it, isn't it?"

'I don't know, we'll see but don't count on it." Chang, curious but reserved, said to the boy.

Conquering his usual hesitation, Chang pushed the button which suddenly caused the whole uplink to activate. The team could only look dumbstruck as they saw all of the lights of the facility flash up and all of the controls become lit up as if to signal that they were useable. Outside, one could have seen the uplink illuminate up before shooting a light into the sky.

"What? What just happened?" Vincent, in shock, asked.

"I don't know how, but this device could be our best chance of survival." Michael replied.

CHAPTER 17: CONTACTING HOME

Up around the highly fortified coastal city of Tromso, the situation was stable. Vast cargo ships travelled into and out of the docks to drop off more supplies and provisions which were then shipped via magnetic rails down south to supply the Terran army on the continent. Such trains would have passed by the simple but distinct triangularly shaped Arctic cathedral that stood out among the other buildings. The inhabitants went about their daily life, sometimes looking up to see squadrons of Terran fighters swooping above the city. Having just got itself restocked and resupplied, the *Tungsten* had just taken off and was on the move again. In the control room, an officer noticed something unusual on the radar.

"Colonel Jethro! Colonel Jethro, sir! We've got a signal from an old beacon!"

Rushing over to the radar, Jethro couldn't help but smirk.

"Contact that uplink! I think I know exactly who it is!" Jethro said.

* * *

Back at the uplink, Michael looked at the radar and received a call.

"Colonel? Is that you, sir?" He said as he pressed his hand against the communicator attached to his ear, "This is Captain Michael Faulkner, Captain of Team Orca...we read you loud and clear!"

"This is the *Tungsten*...now that we have confirmed proof of your survival, we're sending a dropship to your location...hang on tight boys! The Cavalry is on its way!!"

All of the team were relieved upon hearing the news, Zach especially, as he could finally return Dimitri to his parents. But the cheering ended when the alarms went red and a massive quantity of blips appeared on radar. Their signal had also signalled the robots, and they were coming in fast with a large expeditionary force.

***

Back on the *Tungsten*, the officers observed the holographic map with increased worry as they saw the machine army coming towards the uplink. One officer spoke to Jethro, asking

"Sir? What are your orders?"

"Alert the cavalry, bring heavy ordnance....and get me my suit!!"

"Your suit sir? What do you mean?" The officer asked, surprised by the order.

"What do you think I mean, soldier...I'm going out to see that this gets done properly!"

The relief force began to board their dropships, loading heavy equipment onto the vessels as they proceeded to board them. Jethro himself was now clad in armour as he readied his rifle. Then Rufus spotted Jethro entering the dropship.

"Good Lord. The man must be mad."

Rufus observed the boarding process from the bridge. He was still needed on the bridge of the flying fortress so he couldn't afford to join them.

"Then again, it's war. Sometimes madness, not sanity, keeps civilisation secure and preserved" He said to himself as he brooded over what he had seen.

* * *

Meanwhile back at the uplink, the team were relieved at the fact that they were finally found.

"Wait a minute, lads! It is not over yet!" Michael said when he noticed the look on their faces.

The men stopped any potential celebration and everyone's faces dropped as they looked up to Michael.

"Guys, I know what you're thinking, and I apologise for spoiling your excitement." Michael began. "However, our signal was strong, too strong and it attracted a machine army to our location! As we know, machines rely on numbers. They will be five times our numbers and they will have their armoured divisions supporting them!"

"But Jethro knows that we are here, sir, he will send a relief force to support us, won't he?"

"Yes, Alexi, he will! Very well then lads, we know what to do...if we can hold out, we get the cavalry...if we don't...we make sure that our defeat will not be an easy victory for them, understood, boys?"

"We got the drill, sir!"

"Good! Then let's move out!"

Outside the uplink, the machine army had arrived. Giant armoured carriers deployed regiments of heavily armoured robotic soldiers. However, the team stuck to the corridors, ready to hold the line against the incoming machines. They chose a corridor to make their stand because of the compressed space which the machines would have to cram themselves into, without any aerial or heavy support. The machines went up the corridor towards where the team was waiting.

They waited for the oncoming machines, waiting till the machines were close enough for their weapons to have an effect on them. As he heard the clanking of robotic feet, Dimitri spoke to Zach asking,

"Zach, what do we do now?"

"Stay here and let me do the dirty work, alright!"

Dimitri nodded. Zach went down into the corridor with his comrades. It wasn't long before they were blasting the machine hordes. First Dermot used his sniper rifle to take out any small UAVs trying to fly ahead of the horde, then Dia and Alexi barraged their mobile self-propelled turrets with rocket launchers. In the process one of the missiles hit a flamethrower bot, setting off his tank and causing it to explode, destroying several bots in the process. Chang and Zach took out robotic soldiers with their assault rifles while Michael used a shotgun to take out the bots that came closest. It wasn't long before the bots realised that they were heading for slaughter. They retreated from the corridor.

"Eh…is that it?" Zach asked Michael as he saw what he believed to be the bots retreating.

"No, it's not, Zach! They're not retreating, they're going off to find more corridors!"

"How will we know which corridor they're coming?"

"We won't, we'll split up to scout out different corridors…if things get too hot, we'll fall back to the central room…from there we just hold our ground, throw everything we've got at them! Fight till we're using our fists!"

As planned the team scouted out different areas but in each corridor the robots were coming in full force. Zach and Dermot barely stood their ground in the corridor in which they encountered a troop of drones. As Zach fired back, Dermot threw a smoke grenade down the corridor. This disorientated the targeting systems of the drones allowing the two to make their escape. The two managed to make it to the main room where the rest of the team were waiting. They too had encountered the machines in the corridors, and they started to entrench themselves. They used the tattered computers and other scattered remains in the area to build up barricades. It was at these barricades that they would hold their positions.

What ensued next was a gritty battle to the bitter end, where scores of robots fell at first. But after that, the team's firearms ran out of ammo and, after that, they ran out of grenades. Eventually the Alpha Squad team were reduced to fighting with knives, the butt ends of their guns and even their fists. A pile of mangled robots started to gather within the centre of the uplink but that didn't scare the machines. The machines had no conscience or heart which also meant that they had no fear. As a result, the piles of their fallen comrades did not intimidate them, so they pressed on with their attack.

As Alpha Squad started to tire out, they did everything to stay alive, even yanking at the wires of the robotic soldiers' throats to shut them down. They were soaked with sweat and they felt their bones aching with pain, but they held out. They were not going down without a fight.

* * *

This was the moment that it seemed hopeless. But then outside, at least eight dropships bristling with heavy ordnance bombarded the armoured machine carriers destroying them. Seeing the dropships attacking their armoured forces, a squadron of heavy fighter drones swooped into attack the dropships. However, the dropships were escorted by fighter jets. These sleek curved winged aircraft engaged with the drones, shooting them down. As a result of this interception, the drones were not able to shoot down the dropships, allowing them to touch down on the ground to deploy the troops. The troops came armed with a vast array of heavy equipment that tore through the attacking machines as they went up into the corridors of the uplink. Jethro himself, now clad in body armour, personally led a Legionnaire squadron up into the corridors to relieve the team of machines.

"Colonel Jethro?" Michael said, surprised by the sight of his elderly commander.

"You think I'm too old to fight, Captain? Follow me to the dropships, you boys deserve a rest!"

The group followed the rest of the Legionnaires to the perimeter that the dropships created and went into the lead dropship which finally took off for Tromso. Zach couldn't help but sigh with relief. Everyone was relieved. The fleet of dropships continued to make their journey. Any drones that tried to pursue them were shot down by escorting fighter aircraft.

* * *

The sun was starting to sink down, darkening the sky as the dropships flew above the skies. They proceeded to make their journey to Tromso, activating their spotlights as the moon floated up into the air. The moon glowed in the night sky, looking at the vessels as they flew above the vast wasteland below them that had become known as the "Badlands".

Zach held onto Dimitri as the dropship lifted them away from the uplink. The wind was no longer blowing in their face as the ramp had been closed. He looked around and saw all of the squad having their long-earned sleep. From now on it was just a Heli trip to Tromso. Exhausted and drained of energy, Zach started to fall asleep. It was then that he thought of all that had happened. He was actually surprised at how intact he was.

After all, he had been in battle, he had been in the Badlands, he survived a chlorine gas attack and the attack of a mutant squid. Yet in spite of all that, he survived.

Both the gas attack and the squid had one thing in common, it was Zach's teammates that had saved him from certain death. Thinking on all that happened to him, Zach was relieved that he didn't have to soldier through this nightmare alone. Regardless of what happened, he had his team and he could rely on them. Also, he had gained experience and competence from this endeavour which meant that his team could rely on him. Nevertheless, his old life refused to leave him alone and gradually he drifted into another dream. It was of the time he murdered the brat to defend his brother. He was being pursued by the police.

Zach quickly rushed down the back alleys towards the bar where his mother worked. He only had his jeans, brown laced boots and leather jacket on him, and he took Phil by the hand. They ran as quickly as they could as the two police cars came to a halt. Terran policemen, dressed in dark grey uniforms and peakless caps, followed them down the alley. The dogs which they had brought howled and barked as they chased the boys.

The gang who had ganged up on Zach and Phil had long run away as their leader was dead.

They knew that if Zach couldn't provide evidence that he was acting in self-defence, he would possibly receive a death sentence.

"Zach? Where are we going??" Phil asked his brother as they ran.

"We're going to the bar...and that's it."

"But wait? You've been accused of murder and you're going to have a drink?"

"No...I'll explain everything later...come on...whatever has to

happen to me...I don't want you to see it!!"

Zach and Phil continued to run until they finally reached the bar.

* * *

Valentine was working inside as normal when Phil and Zach burst in, panting. She stood there confused as Zach rushed towards her.

"Mom??"

"Zach...what are you doing bringing Phil here...I told you to look after him and that I'd be back by this evening...alright?"

"No...Mom...listen to me... You need to take Phil... that's why I came here!!"

Fear displayed on Zach's face as his sapphire blue eyes locked with hers. Hearing the police car siren wailing in the background she grew pale.

"Zach...what is going on here?"

"Mom...I'll explain everything later...just take Phil and go home...I don't want him to see what happens next...you need to trust me."

"Of course, I trust you, but explain..."

The doors burst open and they heard a deep, booming voice bellow across the room.

"Zach Harker!!! You're summoned to the police station!! I suggest you stand down and come with us!!!!"

Hearing the voice, Phil quickly ran behind the counter beside Valentine while the customers looked on in fear as standing at the door were three police officers. Two of them were pointing pistols at Zach. Meanwhile, the barkeeper came out.

"Valentine? What is going on here??" He said when he caught sight of the police.

"James, please..."

"The police...why are they here?"

Zach was pale with fear...shivers ran up his spine while his heart thumped like regimental drums. However, he breathed in and turned to face the lead police officer.

"Hands behind your head boy!!! Let's get this over with!!!" The

officer ordered.

"Okay...just let me say goodbye to my family first." Zach said.

The officer had little sympathy.

"David...take this boy to the back seat...we'll do the questioning for this murder at the station."

David nodded as he and his colleague violently grabbed onto Zach. Zach struggled at first...feeling the pain of the handcuffs being fastened around his hands as he yelled back at the officers.

"Sir, you've got to listen to me!!! I'm not the aggressor!!! Those fuckers ganged up on me and Phil...I was acting in self-defence!!!"

However, David used his taser on Zach, causing the boy to collapse. Phil clung onto his mother who looked on in pure shock as the two policemen picked up Zach and dragged him out of the bar.

"You stay here until I come back...okay, Honey?" Valentine, still confused herself, said to Phil.

Phil shivered and looked in confusion, however he nodded.

"Good boy," Valentine said.

As she pursued the police, James followed her.

"Hey...Valentine...where do you think you're going?"

"Stay with Phil, James...I'll be back in a few minutes."

"Valentine...Hey Valentine, that's not a good idea...not even with your pleading will you convince the police to let Zach go!!"

Valentine however continued to follow the police.

"Wait?? Tom?? I need to speak to you!!"

The leader of the troop of police looked back at her, scowling.

"Okay...you got my attention...what do you want with me?"

"Tom, if there is one thing, I do know about the situation is that if Zach killed somebody...it wasn't without provocation!!"

"You weren't on the scene, Ma'am...how would you know that?"

"Tom, I'm his mother...don't you think I'd know my own son after raising him for eighteen years??"

"Well from what I saw in the front garden of your house was Zach wriggling the knife out of some poor bastard and stabbing him!!"

"And seeing a bunch of weirdos in the front garden cornering two boys didn't raise any questions in you...no?? You just charged the victim that fought back?? What sort of law is this? I thought Terran law was supposed to be just!"

"*Valentine!!! Go back to the bar...If you have any points to make on this situation you make them with your lawyer, not me...I'm just doing my job!! Now good day!! Terran law doesn't take chances!!*"

He got into the car with his colleagues and drove off to the station.

CHAPTER 18: GETTING BACK TO CIVILIZATION

Zach woke up after that dream, hearing the noise of the engines of the dropship. He looked around him to see the rest of the group waking up. Day time had come. Michael, having woken up, was now looking down at his watch. It was half seven in the morning. Sitting up on the bench, Zach looked down at Dimitri who was fast asleep. He called over to Michael.

"Sir?"

"Please...you can just call me Michael...you've earned it by now. You may have been a poor warrior when we first had you...but you are a good brother...that is enough to make you one of us. Now, tell me what want to know?"

"Just looking at this kid...I couldn't help but wonder...do you have children of your own?"

"No, I don't."

"Not even a wife?"

"No, I don't have a wife to miss me either!"

"No wife, no kids? Michael, is it really true that Legionnaires are not allowed to get married?"

"No... we're not supposed to marry."

"Why not...isn't that unfair? I mean what if we fall in love."

"No... We've been modified to fight and to kill...we'd make poor husbands...we'd have too much stimulation and adrenaline running through our bodies; our bodies are built for killing not loving. A woman would have a healthier life with a mortal man, Zach. Our lives are on the battlefield, we would have no room for a life outside of that."

Zach didn't speak anymore. However, as he thought back on what he had just been taught he felt strangely relieved. He might be the runt of the squad, but now he was part of the team.

✻ ✻ ✻

Eventually, the dropship landed in the fortified garrison that watched over the city of Tromso. The patrolling troops and the men in the bar heard the sound of the dropships touching down.

"Do you hear that? It sounds like a dropship!"

"It's Alpha Squad, we've just heard about them on the radio! They have returned home. They're still alive!"

"What? Praise God, come on, their constant survival is an act worth of celebration in and of itself!"

The men all came over to surround the fleet of dropships as they touched down onto a landing pad. Coming down from the ramp, Zach kept Dimitri close to him as he and the rest of the team were cheered on. Much to his surprise he and his companions were given a hero's welcome, by both fully fledged Legionnaires and new meats. The Home Guardsmen couldn't help but smile at seeing their most hardened veterans back. As this hero's welcome extended beyond the garrison and into the streets, some of the civilians had heard the cheering, notably Anya and Nicholas, and came over to see what was going on. Nicholas spotted Dimitri and was stunned.

"It cannot be...Oh God...Anya... I'll be back in a moment!"

Struck with joy and disbelief at the sight of his child, Nicolas and ran off through the crowd.

Anya couldn't hold back so she followed Nicholas. Nicholas desperately and excitedly rushed through the crowd of cheering soldiers. Dimitri, seeing Nicholas, rushed towards his father. Zach tagged along quickly behind.

"Dimitri!!" Nicholas started to say. "Oh, damn it...I thought you were dead!! I am so sorry!! I lost my grip after tripping...I cannot find the words to express how sorrowful I am over this mess."

Nicholas passed Dimitri to Anya, who snuggled him close. He then turned to face Zach.

"If I were a rich man...I could reward you with all sorts of finery...but as a father...and a refugee...I really can't imagine how I can possibly show my gratitude...but all I can say is thank you...Legionnaire!"

Then, much to Zach's surprise, he threw his arms around the

Legionnaire. Taken aback, Zach just hugged him back.

"You don't need to thank me, sir. I don't need any reward, I merely doing my job."

Having seen the boy returned to his parents, Zach was about to leave, only for Dimitri to shout after him.

"Zach...wait!"

Zach turned around and walked towards Anya who lowered Dimitri down so he could walk towards Zach. Zach knelt down as Dimitri approached him. Curious and concerned, Zach spoke to Dimitri.

"What is it?"

"I just...want to say thanks...and goodbye...It just feels..."

"Difficult? I kinda felt the same when it came to leaving my family to join the Legion...whether you do...that's your own decision...not mine...you move on with life alright? Stay strong and try to do what's right."

"Okay...thanks...brother."

The two shared a tearful embrace before Dimitri went back to his mother. Zach felt quite emotional as he saw the boy and his family smile at him as they walked away. After all, he had been with the boy for weeks during their time in the Badlands and he was used to seeing him. Zach suddenly felt a hand on his back. He turned around to see Michael.

"Come on Zach...he's with his own people now...you've done the right thing."

"Okay...but it just feels..."

"Difficult? The life of a warrior is deeply envied...but it is full of difficulty...sometimes the right decision is the hardest one to make! But when you make the right choice, you feel a virility in you that is stronger than that which you feel after slaying the greatest beast!"

Zach nodded as he came back with Michael and the rest of the team. As sad as Zach felt, he knew in his heart that he had done the right thing in bringing Dimitri back to his parents. He was also glad that he made himself useful during the mission. It may not have meant that much in relation to the war overall, in all its grand scale, and it might not be recorded in the history books as a fantastic achievement, but for Zach, taking that kid under his wing allowed him to cope with his own fears and anxieties about his new life in the Legion. It was something for him to be proud of.

* * *

Later that day, Zach rang home. He wasn't as nervous or as scared as he was before the events of St Petersburg. However, he was now feeling a strange mix of sadness and satisfaction. To be honest with himself Zach couldn't really describe how he was feeling. All he knew was that he was emotional in some way. He tried to maintain control over his emotions as he spoke down the phone.

"Hello? Mom? Phil? It's me, Zach."

"Zach? You're alive?"

"Yes Mom...I'm alive...and I'm back, probably being sent to die again...how's Phil?"

"Phil's still in bed...do you want me to pass the phone to him, Zach?"

"Eh...Okay."

"Come on Zach, we were both deeply worried about whether you would survive or not...I'm sure Phil would be glad to hear your voice again...he's not heard it since you joined!"

"Alright, you might as well...but I'm not exactly the boy I was."

Valentine went up to Phil, and gently woke him up to give him the phone. Phil was nervous at first but he eventually grew courageous enough to speak.

"Zach?"

"Hey, Phil...do you still remember me?"

"I remember your face...what's it like to be in the army?"

"Not a place for a little boy...you stay at home with Mommy alright?"

"Don't you have friends over there?"

"You know what...I actually do."

"Really?"

"Yeah, and your buddies will be the best thing about army

life."

"Okay, that's nice, you'll visit us someday right...I mean when you get the chance."

"Don't worry Phil, I'll try to get back to you...goodbye."

Phil then passed the phone back to his mother.

"Zach...are you allowed to come home? Because if you can, you're always welcome home."

"I've got a war to fight, Mom...but thanks...if I'm free I'll try! I love you, Mom."

"I love you too, Zach, goodbye."

"Goodbye, Mom."

Zach sighed after he put down the phone. Saying goodbye before going to school was one thing but saying goodbye before going back to fight was the hardest thing to say, simply because you may never come back.

"Is that your family you're talking to?" Dermot asked.

"Yeah...I guess you don't have any family to come back to, do you not?"

"Aye...not really...me and my sister were forced to resort to crime on the streets of Glasgow, where as a city wrecked by amphibious invasions, enforcement of Terra's laws was laxer. Gangs dominated and corrupted the city. The home guard was as much at war with the gangs as it was with the attacking machines. I had to steal to feed my little sister. I got caught, joined the Legion to escape the death penalty. Don't worry, my sister was able to start a living for herself with the compensation. She then went on to become a doctor in Inverness."

"I see, we're like icebergs Dermot, there's more to us than what might one initially see."

"From what I heard about what you said to Alexi at the bar, you were lucky when it came to your mother."

"What do you mean?"

"Zach, you were born to a good woman, and by the sounds of it, she loves you well!"

"Yeah...I feel that as well...and I'm not the only one."

"I know."

Their business down on the surface was done, with Dimitri

back safely with his parents. The team returned via dropship to the *Tungsten* to wait for new orders.

CHAPTER 19: SLAYING THE IRON MONSTER

Back on the flying fortress, Zach had a hard time sleeping after all that had happened. He was by then used to having Dimitri around and he was used to sleeping in the open air. There were times when he thought as if he was still sleeping in his sleeping bag by the campfire only to wake up under the bedsheets in his bed.

As a result of these dreams, he couldn't sleep properly so he heaved himself out from his bunk and headed out for the bar so that he could reunite with his squad. Much to his surprise, everybody had taken off their helmets and caps in his presence and cheered him when he showed up. This was followed by a round of applause as he slowly came towards the bar counter. It was obvious that his very survival had filled the men with pride.

As he approached the counter, some distinctly Irish tune was playing in the background.

"Well, hello, you're Zach?" The barkeep said to him.

"Yes sir, that's me!"

"The boys of Alpha Squad have been telling stories about your bravery! How you went almost suicidally into the underground of a battered Saint Petersburg for the sake of a kid! By the end of this war, you could become a folk hero!"

"Oh please, thank my comrades! They saved me from a big ugly squid. The bards should be singing about them not me. Still, a glass of Jameson would do nicely!"

The barkeep took out a glass and then took out a bottle of Jameson. Opening the bottle, he filled up the glass. After paying the barkeep, Zach walked over to the rest of the troops. All of the men were drinking a wide variety of alcoholic beverages, ranging from vodka and Guinness to rum and beer. Michael then clasped a glass of beer in his hand as, shouting, he made an announcement to the crowd.

"A toast! A toast for the human race and its formidable capacity to endure any threat hurled in its path! For God! For

Terra!! For the Legion!!"

The men clinked their glasses together as they yelled as one.

"For God! For Terra!! For the Legion!"

As he drank his Jameson, Zach felt a surge of warmth, energy and pride slowly fill his veins. He was finally part of the Legion; he wasn't just a boy among men, he was one of them. These were the same men who had seen him as a little twerp. Now they showed him proper respect and he didn't gain this out of glory or by ripping apart the entire robotic army all by himself. He received the adulation because it was he who saw Dimitri home; because he took on the responsibility for someone more vulnerable even though it greatly endangered him. That was what it was to be a warrior. There was more to warriorhood than just killing, there was a whole culture of brotherhood, loyalty and duty that made a legionnaire stand out in battle from a machine.

To be called a brother in the Legion was the greatest honour that Zach could have received. Sure, he wasn't anything like Beowulf and probably couldn't rip off Grendel's arm, but he was one of them now.

Now, he drank as one of them, and he engaged in their games, even arm wrestling. It no longer mattered if he won or lost because even though he lost most of his wrestles, it was still fun to take part in such games. No longer did this new world of the Legion feel strange and spooky to him. Rather it gave him a warmth and feeling of security that he had thought he would never feel in a foreign land without his family. He wondered what his father would have thought of him at that moment.

The partying in the bar went on for many hours and it took a long time for Zach and the others to get to sleep that night.

* * *

The following morning, a rumble occurred, a big rumble that shook the ground. The sound of the Black Mouth's feet could be heard for miles, sending vibrations through the streets of the city down below.

Hearing this, the people started to panic. Up in the *Tungsten*, Rufus Thorne was observing the holographic map when he saw the image of the Black Mouth heading towards the Norwegian coast. Following the Black Mouth was what looked to be a large machine naval and airborne force. Rufus Thorne's eyes widened in shock, clearly, the Black Mouth noticed the military concentration that was developing around Tromso. For as a key port city that linked up with Terra's Northern sea routes, Tromso was one of the key ports to supplying the Terran army in Europe. As Thorne taught on this, Jethro appeared beside him and announced.

"Sir! We have reports of the Black Mouth coming. Our outposts can see it for miles! What are our orders?"

"We stand our ground! Alert every military asset in the area to make our stand! We are not shying away from the Black Mouth! It is coming for a fight and it shall get it!"

* * *

Immediately the men got to their positions, preparing the weaponry of their flying fortresses to fight the oncoming army. The flying fortresses turned their enormous guns to face the sea as the Black Mouth's force approached. Down on the ground, squadrons of legionnaires garrisoned the trenches. Supporting them were giant vehicles that ran on two sets of caterpillar tracks which positioned themselves behind the trenches. Although they just looked like rectangular blocks on tracks at first, once they stopped, legs extended from each side of the vehicle that stamped onto the ground, digging the machine into the ground. Emerging on top of the vehicle were rectangular shaped missiles. Beside the launcher was a deck that had a computer and targeting devices which were operated by legionnaires.

Seeing the flying fortresses and the squadrons of fighters flying above them, one of the Legionnaires gave them a salute.

Awaiting in reserve behind the entrenchments were fleets of tanks and armoured cars ready to fill in gaps of the trenches. The trenches themselves were formidable as they were made of pure metal and surrounded by an array of barbed wire. They were fitted with heavy machine guns, artillery pieces, missiles and EMP devices. The Legionnaires and Home Guardsmen stood ready. One of their officers took out his binoculars. Zooming in, the officer could see the machine army as it displayed itself in all its terrifying glory. It comprised several battleships and an array of armoured, amphibious personnel carriers that were ready to deploy thousands of machines. Squadrons of drones and frigates flew above the fleet and smaller ships, equipped with missile launchers to shoot down enemy aircraft, escorted the battleships.

At that moment, the machine battleships were bombarding the trenches, focusing on the main coastal guns. In response to this, the artillery of the Legion and the flying fortresses bombarded the battleships. The battle had begun.

Overseeing the scene from the holographic map, Rufus could see that, for the moment at least, the entrenchments were holding. Two Terran naval squadrons, comprising submarines and destroyers, were moving in a pincer move towards the machine fleet. This surety of victory, however, would not last as the Black Mouth was coming closer and closer to the entrenchments on the beaches. This was something Rufus knew all too well. Seeing what was unfolding, Rufus gave Jethro his orders.

"Colonel Jethro! I demand to see Alpha Squad right now! I've got a mission for them!"

"Yes, sir!"

The alert lights flashed red, causing everyone in Alpha Squad to head to the armoury.

"Wait, what's happening?" Zach, confused and disorientated, asked Michael.

"It's here! Here to finish what it started!!"

"Oh no... you mean...the Black Mouth...it's attacking Tromso...what about the civilian population?"

"All the more reason why we can't waste time...Zach come on!!"

As the rest of the Team were gearing up for the oncoming battle, Jethro approached Michael.

"Captain Michael Faulkner...I need you to gather your squad and head to the control room!"

"Understood, sir! Boys, follow me!"

* * *

Shortly after, the whole of Alpha Squad were assembled in the control tower of the *Tungsten*. There, Michael and Jethro went to meet Rufus in the control room. When they arrived, Rufus was looking at a holographic map, watching the progress of the preparations for the battle taking place off the coast of Tromso.

"Captain Faulkner...so glad you're here...I have a special mission for you!!" Rufus said to Michael when he spotted him.

"What do you mean sir?"

"You know the Black Mouth, whose titanium structure is impervious to any form of kinetic weaponry, is heading to Tromso? It obviously can't take on our offensive in Eurasia head on so it has decided to attack us from behind by cutting off our ports to the Atlantic."

"That's why we are here...what do you need us to do?"

"Captain...I need your team to infiltrate the Black Mouth and reach the central node...there are strange messages coming from it...that make it impossible to hack...going into the Black Mouth's core will bring great difficulties but shutting it down from the inside is the only way to stop it!! The machine's generator emits so much heat that it requires large ventilators! These ventilators are large enough for people to fit through! Mind you, the machines will be using every method to stop you! Our map has depicted a large force that is escorting the Black Mouth."

"You're sending us on a suicide mission...aren't you?" Michael asked, having absorbed what Throne was asking him and his men to do.

"Captain Faulkner...we will minimise the dangers of the mission by sending our own armies to attack the robotic force...provide a distraction...keep them away from you as long as possible! But this is for the common good of humanity and all living organisms. Are you ready to sacrifice yourself for the greater good? FOR TERRA! For Mankind!!"

Michael paused before he replied.

"I cannot promise you success in this mission, Commander Thorne! But I will not let you down sir!"

* * *

Later Michael joined his squad as they went into the dropship. They took off into the heat of a big battle between the Legion's flying fortresses, dropships and strike craft and the machines defending the Black Mouth. They had barely taken off when a missile narrowly missed their dropship.

Zach could feel chills running down his spine. This was the Black Mouth they were leaving to face, the most powerful machine ever created by humanity. It was a machine built to end World War 3, but it only prolonged the war, transforming what was a power struggle between nations and into a war between humanity and machines.

At that moment, Zach and his friends were heading off to confront it. He looked around him. Everyone had their helmets and gas masks on. Their discipline kept their emotions in check while they clasped their weapons in their gloved hands. Zach did his best to discipline his own fears and anxieties.

It felt like everything was coming to an end for Zach, however. Everything in his life, from his birth to his father's death to his conscription had all led to this moment. The very thought that history would be decided here made Zach scared.

"Eh, fellas? Is this it? Is this the end?" Zach asked, nervously.

Upon hearing this question, Michael stood up, and much to Zach's awe, his comrades stood up also. He joined them. Michael started to speak.

"Don't ever ask if this is the end. This is not the end! Nor the beginning of the end...this is the end of the beginning!"

Hearing this, the pilots upped their radio frequencies so that Michael's speech could be heard booming throughout loudspeakers and radios. It could be heard on the flying fortress, near where the soldiers, in their trenches, battled against the machines, in navies gathered around Tromso, and where the armoured platoons were heading towards the trenches to support their troops. Michael continued his speech.

"All of my life....and all of your lives have come to this point! There is no going home...no turning from battle...once you are in the Legion...there is no end to fighting! Boys...I am just as scared as you are of dying...but we all must put away our fear...because no matter how bloody the battle becomes...no matter how hopeless it is...no matter how many comrades and brothers we lose...know that a soldier's greatest comfort and finest honour...is to have his friends by his side! Know that a civilian's greatest comfort is to have their homes free from the chaos of violence! In the end no matter how bloody it gets; how hopeless it becomes, there are some things that are just worth fighting for!"

There was mass cheering among all the legionnaires on the ground who immediately continued to fight even harder against the machines. It was as if they had a rejuvenated spirit, strengthened by the speech. It gave them the courage to fight on, no matter how hopeless the situation would get. As they did this, many of them chanted

"FOR TERRA!!"

The Home Guard and the Legionnaires then began to chant louder and louder.

"FOR TERRA!! FOR MANKIND!!"

This was, after all, the kind of warfare that they had fought for, that they had been modified for, that they had trained for, that they were born for. No matter how nightmarish the battle would become, they knew they would hold their ground.

* * *

The Black Mouth came into view. This time however, Zach was not afraid to see the nightmarish, eight-legged robot that they called the Black Mouth. It was as if the speech had cleansed the last

143

vestiges of fear that he was feeling.

Besides, the monster's armies were having a hard time battling the inspired legionnaires. The ventilation tubes on the machine were so big that an elephant could slide down them. It was these ventilation systems that kept the Black Mouth cool because of the sheer heat that the machine was generating.

The dropship hovered over one of them. The pilots signalled to the team that they were over a vent. This prompted the men to stand up and head towards the ramp of the dropship so they would be ready to jump out. As the ramp opened, they felt a blast of air on their faces. This was chilling their bodies but not destroying their spirit or resilience. As they went down the ramp, Dermot spoke to Zach.

"Ready...or scared?"

"Oh, I'm definitely scared...but if it's for the good of Terra and its people...I'm ready!!"

"That's it, laddie!"

Zach was still afraid about confronting his terrors within the chambers of the Black Mouth, but he was ready to do his duty for his people, for Terra.

For Terra was a nation state infamous for its lethal punishments and its contempt for weakness, especially among its own people. Yet it was this very force that was standing between civilised society and the machines.

When the lights in the hull flashed bright green, the team rushed down the ramp and skydived into the ventilation tube which they went sliding down through. The slide slowed their fall until they fell into a corridor illuminated by red lighting. The men picked themselves up and started to look around them. Zach was curious about the sight of the corridors.

"Okay...this is like the corridors you see in a submarine...I thought this thing was robotic!" Zach said.

"I know...be careful...there might be machines around the place!!" Chang replied.

Conscious that they were in machine-infested territory, Dia snapped.

"Chang, if there are machines around then let's keep our

voices down."

"Gentlemen! Come into a circle!"

The team circled around Michael.

"Listen up lads, we are inside the Black Mouth...the central core has a heavy garrison surrounding it. Vincent, Alexi, Chang, Dermot and Dia, I need you to strike attacks on the machine's leg sockets; this will cause trouble, create a distraction. Zach and I will be headed for the core. The rest of you, stay together; when we shut down the machine you immediately proceed for the vents and climb up onto the platform where a dropship will pick you up!!"

None of the team liked what Michael had said. Vincent spoke up.

"What...what about you? Michael, you've got us through almost every fucking nightmare that we've been plunged into. And what about Zach? He's done things that I would never have the conscience to do like going in alone for the sake of finding a boy. Are we just to have the two of you die?"

"Gentlemen!" Michael began. "I could never have reached the status that I am at now had I never known you...it is your actions as a whole that has brought us here!! We may not have families waiting for us...but we have each other! Understood?"

"Understood sir!"

The men proceeded with their plans, which resulted in a lot of corridor battles against numerous heavy assault bots and turrets. Still the team's ability to coordinate as a unit allowed them to gradually punch through the corridors of the Black Mouth. At one point, the team found a perfectly clean corridor with no turrets or machines. It seemed that the team was in for a clean walk, but Chang stopped them.

"Wait! Too easy. Where are their guards?"

Aware that something was not right, Dermot took out a knife and flung it across the floor. Suddenly an enormous rectangular shaped stamp with spikes slammed against the floor.

"Jesus, if we make a move, that will be the fate of one of us! Any plans, lads?" Dermot asked.

"I'll get out a grenade and you'll get another one of your

knives, I have a plan that might work." Dia replied.

Dermot got another knife while Dia got out one of his anti-tank grenades. Dermot threw the knife, causing the stamp to come down again while Dia threw the grenade above the stamp. As the grenade stuck to the spiked stamp, it went back up. Knowing what would happen next, Dia told the others to run so they fled, and, as they did, that whole part of the corridor blew up, putting a hole in the Black Mouth.

CHAPTER 20: THE CORE

Electricity sparked all around the tattered room and the wind came gushing in, forcing the team to cling on. As they struggled to climb across the wall to get to the rest of the corridor, Vincent spoke.

"Well, look on the bright side, we've managed to avoid being squashed like jelly!"

"Don't get your hopes up, Vincent, we might have more traps to deal with." Dia replied.

Eventually, after a long, gruelling, uphill struggle against machines and traps, the team succeeded in sabotaging a joint and, as a result, the Black Mouth started to jerk. The sight of the Black Mouth just slightly jerking caused squadrons of drones to come back to the defence of the monstrous metallic titan. Dropships and fighter aircraft often pursued them and engaged them in battle. This wasn't easy because the Black Mouth started using its miniguns and missiles to shoot down the Terran aircraft that came too close to it. This forced Terran squadrons to fly away from the enormous robotic machine.

Back at the *Tungsten*, Rufus Thorne and Jethro were looking at the holographic map. Things were going much better this time as the map was getting greener and greener, indicating that they were gradually starting to beat the machine army. However, Jethro noticed on the screen that aircraft that tried to support the team in destroying the Black Mouth were being picked off.

"Sir, our aircraft are being taken out by drones and the Black Mouth's guns!" He said to Throne.

"Damn it! Idiots, they were to draw the machine army away from the Black Mouth! Order them to call off their attack on the Black Mouth! Their retreat should help lure some machines away from the Black Mouth and towards our flying fortresses!"

"Yes, sir!"

* * *

Down on the Norwegian coast, the machines were still making their attack on the beaches. Submarines were at work torpedoing their command ships. Guarding the main beach head was the legionnaire detachment of the flying fortresses *Kirov*. Armed to the teeth, tough, hardened and ruthless, these soldiers were the strongest of all the Terran legions and their flying fortress was the largest of all the flying fortresses, yet it was still only half the size of the Black Mouth.

Its men had come from the lands of Eastern Europe, a people who had to deal with the machine hordes on a daily basis so they had already grown up with the expectation that they would be in the Legion.

They were able to hold a beach single handily with the support of their flying fortress. This caused the machine offensive to be stalled before they could even reach any populated areas. At long last, other detachments, particularly the Scandinavian Fenrir, Jormungandr and Nidhogg battalions arrived to relive the *Kirov* regiment. That being said, it was a battle that already had cost the Terrans a significant number of their troops and machines.

* * *

Meanwhile, Zach and Michael had their own struggles as they toiled through the host of traps and enemies that guarded the central core. The narrow corridors which were mostly dark and only dimly lit with red lighting made for a claustrophobic experience for the two men to fight through.

They approached the doors to the central node. Zach readied his rifle as he was expecting something to shoot out at him but instead, gas spewed out through the slits surrounding the door. Even though Zach was fully geared and equipped, with his mask firmly on him, the sight of thick chlorine gas quickly engulfing him caused him to panic and stumble to the ground.

He could barely see beyond his gloved hands which caused him to feel even more vulnerable. Once again, he was confronted by the very force that killed his father and it reduced him to pathetic levels of weakness and hopelessness.

"Zach! Zach!" He heard Michael's voice shouting at him.

"The gas! The fucking gas!"

"Zach, don't shrink away, confront it! Confront it, damn you!" Michael replied.

Zach started to stand up, breathing in and out.

"Sir, I can't see you, it's too thick!"

"Don't fear the gas, Zach! You have your mask and you have your oxygen! It won't kill you!"

Michael came over to Zach, grasping onto him to steady him. Zach could see Michael and their eyes locked in contact with each other. It was then that Zach found in himself a renewed vigour to persist and he stood firmly on his own two feet. Zach continued to breath as he clasped his rifle in his hand. Michael patted Zach's shoulder.

"Keeping breathing Zach and stay calm. You have the equipment to keep you safe so don't be scared. Alright?"

"Yes, Captain!"

"That's it, Zach! Now come on, we have a job to do!"

Zach and Michael approached the big door. There was no way to open it manually, so they put explosives in place, set a timer and ran from the door. The resulting explosion blasted through it. With that done, they slowly entered the central core, only to find that the wires that were attached to the central node looked like nerve cords.

Confused and horrified by this, Zach approached the node and found a brain inside. It was being kept within a container filled with some sort of liquid and it had all sorts of wires attached to it. Seeing something like that filled Zach with a strange feeling of pity for the organism in front of him.

"So, this is why it could never be hacked yet it could hack others...its central AI was organic!! It's bulging like it's trying to get some sort of message!" Michael said as he observed the brain.

"Did we ever know this?"

"The Chinese kept the development of the Black Mouth top secret during the Third World War, so that the other great nations couldn't replicate the technology. Remember the Black Mouth was built to turn the tide in the war! Its role was to end the war once and for all."

"But it is alive...it's got a memory...and a brain!"

"Zach, we must shut it down...that brain is entirely in agony! It must be done...we must shut it down!! We must end its misery...for the greater good...sacrifices must be made!"

Though he felt a strange remorse for the abomination as he now realised that it had a brain, Zach also felt a deep hatred and contempt for the Black Mouth. After all, it was the Black Mouth who controlled the machine hordes. Without it, he would still have his father and he would never have had to live his life in fear. He gritted his teeth as he knew that he had his duty; it had all come down to that moment.

Zach knelt down and, grabbing a plug, spoke softly.

"I'm deeply sorry for what has been done to you. But this is for God, my people and for Terra."

Zach yanked the plug out causing all the lighting to flicker and rumbles to occur.

* * *

Making their journey through the already darkly lit corridors, the team started to feel the rumbling and the instability of the Black Mouth. Noticing the flickering lights, Vincent tapped his side shoulder and immediately contacted Michael.

"Captain? What in the name of God is going on here?"

"Gentlemen! Zach and I have just commenced the shutdown of the Black Mouth...it is in the process of self-destruction!!"

"What?"

"Just get off the robot! It is in the process of self-destruction! We'll catch up with you later!!"

As the team made their way to one of the ventilation systems and started to climb back up, they could hear a deep voice from the intercom saying

"Self-destruction in five minutes and counting!"

Fortunately for the team, a dropship had noticed the stumbling Black Mouth, so it had returned and was hovering above the ventilation system. This allowed the team to make it off the robot and onto the ramp of the dropship, but Michael and Zach were still inside. As the dropship hovered over the area, the team could see from the ramp of the dropship that the robot was in the process of collapsing into the coastline and a sense of dread filled their hearts because they also knew that their leader was trapped in the machine.

There was also the fact that something so big about to blow up in only five minutes was a serious threat to the survival of the whole population in the region. Both Michael and Zach were aware of the threat and they wasted no time in setting out to stop it.　　　In an effort to stop the self-destruction. Michael and Zach climbed back up through the corridors of the machine to its central node which they had just emerged from. At first, Michael and Zach searched for the self-destruction device so that they could sabotage it.

Then they heard the voice announcing that they had only two minutes. Horrified and desperate, the two got their knives out and started to slice through the wires around the central hub of the vessel as the timer constantly ticked down the seconds. Zach was drenched with sweat because any moment could have been his last. The Black Mouth was about to be destroyed and all their efforts to defend the city would be for nothing because when the robot blew up, it would take everything with it. It was at the very last minute that Zach managed to cut a wire linked to the self-destruction system.

An appalling silence ensued as the machine shut down its self-destruction. But it was still going to collapse onto land. Neither of the two had time to celebrate their achievement as they needed to escape.

As they rushed through the corridors of the machine, the imbalance of the Black Mouth caused Michael and Zach to fall down one of the ventilators. In desperation, Michael clung onto one of the handles on the ventilator. He clung onto Zach as well, but the Black Mouth was falling. As the it continued its collapse onto the beach, the soldiers defending the beaches started to flee the area, scrambling to their dropships and heading to the city. Dropships and vehicles fled out of the way as the Black Mouth continued to fall onto the mainland.

Meanwhile, Michael was getting increasingly exhausted as he strained under both his own weight and that of Zach. His grasp on the handle slipped and they both fell. Though they were close enough to the ground to survive, they were still knocked out.

* * *

Vincent got the dropship to follow the collapsing robot as it finally crashed against the shore by the nearby city. He had already lost Hans; he was not going to lose another two-squad member, especially his boss.

The Home Guard and the other legionnaire garrisons fled the city surroundings when they saw the Black Mouth crashing down onto the city. The enormous body of the machine was enough to tear through whole buildings. Then it finally came to a halt. None of the troops could believe their eyes. For laying tattered and slain at their feet was the most terrifying war machine ever created by mortal man.

The dark reign of the Black Mouth had been finally brought to an end.

***

Meanwhile, Dimitri was cuddled up asleep in his mother's arms when he was suddenly woken up by a big crash that took place outside.

"Dad? Did you hear that?" He asked his father.

"I did, Dimitri."

"Then come on, the battle is probably over! Let's get out!"

Nicholas turned pale.

"Dimitri, no! Don't go out...it's not safe! We need to wait for the wardens to tell us!"

"But we don't know when that will be, Dad!"

Dimitri dashed off through the shelter and towards the hatch. Nicholas and Anya dashed straight after him.

They had already gone through the horror of losing their son in Saint Petersburg, they didn't want to go through that again. Dimitri managed to make it to the hatch. He was tired of being underground in a shelter for so long, so he wanted to taste the fresh air.

Despite the warnings of civilians and air raid wardens, Dimitri opened the hatch and went out. He was finally able to feel the fresh cool air of the open after having been underground for so long. To see the natural light was a massive relief for him. He started to walk through the battlefield.

Suddenly he started to feel very small and tiny again. In front of him were the enormous, destroyed remains of the Black Mouth. The huge, arachnid-like metallic monster didn't feel so frightening to Dimitri as it had before now that it was motionless.

All around him was an eerie silence. There were no active machines in sight either. All around him were torn remains of different kinds of machinery, manned and unmanned. There was even a fallen flying fortress in the distance; it was so big that could be seen for miles.

Scattered across the ground were the tattered corpses of Legionnaires and Home Guardsmen, with vicious scars and tears in their body. Up in the sky, he could see several flying fortresses, including the *Tungsten*. They were just hovering in the sky and they were so silent that they looked to Dimitri as if they were in a picture.

At first, he felt nervous about the eerie silence but then he slowly approached the ruins of the Black Mouth, fascinated by what he saw in front of him. He turned around and yelled.

"Hey, there are no more machines...the Black Mouth is dead! It's safe to come up!"

Slowly, civilians began to emerge from their shelters and the soldiers from their trenches in order to see the remains of the enormous machine.

Every human in the area came to observe the Black Mouth. They were overjoyed that a menace which had terrified them for so long was finally destroyed. Dimitri approached closer to the Black Mouth and now he could see its legs up close. More importantly, he could see Michael and Zach lying on the ground; with Michael shielding Zach from most of the debris.

The Alpha Squad dropship soon landed near the wreckage. As soon as the ramp lowered down, the squad exited the dropship and began to approach Michael and Zach. They all had a feeling of dread when they saw the two bodies motionless because they feared the worst for their companions. They stopped when they saw Dimitri approach the bodies of the two. Concerned about both Zach and Michael, Dermot started to approach but Dia stopped him.

"Wait, let the boy wake them up."

"But, Dia, he's our teammate!"

"Dermot, without Zach, the boy would be dead. He owes Zach his life, let him return the favour."

As the team watched, Dimitri climbed on top of Zach and began shaking his body.

"Zach? Zach! It's me, Dimitri...don't go on me, I wouldn't be here with my parents if you and your friends hadn't found me!! Come on, the both of you, don't die...come on, get up! GET UP!"

The little boy tried to shake both Zach and Michael's bodies, but it was no use. His body was too small to make such muscular and physically fit bodies even move an inch.

Nicholas and Anya rushed over to Dimitri.

"Dimitri! Stop it! You're not doing them any good...come on..."

"But they're my friends, I owe them my life!"

"I know but you are too small to have any effect on their bodies! Let's go."

But just as Anya pulled Dimitri back, Zach opened his sapphire-blue eyes.

"Eh, Dimitri is that you?"

Michael stirred as well. Dimitri smiled back at his friend while the rest of the team rushed over to help them up. For their heroism in slaying the Black Mouth and securing victory in what could have been a potential defeat for the human race, all the Legionnaires cheered the squad on and formed a guard of honour for them as they made their way through the ruined streets. All the civilians of both Saint Petersburg and Tromso joined in cheering them on.

A warmth began to pervade Zach's heart. In the heat of the emotion, he felt in this moment, he barely remembered any of the bad things, including how he got to be part of the Legion in the first place.

Even the most powerful squadron of legionnaires, the soldiers of the *Kirov* made way for the team. Eventually Michael raised his fist to signal his team to stop. Turning around the face the gathered crowd of legionnaires, Home Guard soldiers and civilians alike, Michael spoke.

"Ladies and gentlemen!! As you might have noticed! The BLACK MOUTH IS FINISHED!! MY SQUAD BROUGHT AN END TO THIS MONSTROSITY! AND ZACH CAUSED ITS DEMISE!!"

Zach felt stunned in awe and pride as Michael clasped onto his hand and raised it.

"HAIL ZACH HARKER!! HERO OF THE TERRAN LEGIONS!! HERO OF HUMANITY!!!"

CHAPTER 21: THE CONQUERING HERO

A series of deep booming cheers, mainly from the men of the *Kirov* echoed in his ears. Zach felt his cheeks go red with embarrassment, but his heart felt passionate and warm as he was now being treated as a hero by his people. However, as he was only nineteen, he didn't feel ready to have a personality cult that normally followed a hero. Besides, he couldn't have done any of his great deeds without the support of his team. He tried to think for himself as he heard the cheering around him. All of a sudden, he feared that with his own glorification, the efforts of everyone who helped him through this endeavour would be devalued.

Zach raised his hand which immediately caused the crowd to fall silent. Zach gathered his courage to announce to the crowd "Ladies and Gentlemen, I am glad to see you all today and I thank you all for the applause. But I would like to take some time to give credit to my team and I wish to congratulate everyone who took part in the defence of this city and its inhabitants. It takes a lot of courage to go up against a monstrosity like that and I was just as scared as all of you were when I first went into the nightmare that is War. However, I would love to give special honour to my comrades, they helped me survive the defeat of Saint Petersburg, they waited for me when I went off to search for Dimitri and there were times that I could have died in the Badlands had it not been for my team. Ladies and gentlemen, could you all give every one of them a round of applause!"

After that speech, the crowd resumed its applause and cheering. All of the team felt surprised at Zach's speech, but they were all proud.

Not just proud of him but proud of themselves as well, for they had all played an important role in Zach's journey to become a hero of the Terran people.

✳ ✳ ✳

Meanwhile, Michael realised that there was just one more thing to do.

"Give me your radio, soldier, I need to send a message to Rufus Thorne." He said to a radio operator.

There was wide cheering from the flying fortresses because many of the crew could see the ruins of the Black Mouth. This was one of the biggest victories that they had in years. At first Rufus was confused at what all the cheering was about. For years, the Terrans assumed that there was nothing that could bring down the Black Mouth and now such an act had just been done. Jethro then approached Rufus Thorne.

"Sir? It seems that the Black Mouth has been destroyed!"

"Yes, do we know if Michael or any of his squad are alive or not?"

"One of our officers picked up a radio message. We believe it's from Captain Faulkner!"

"Thank god! Come Colonel Jethro, let us hear he what he was to say."

Rufus and Jethro approached a control panel and asked an officer to play the radio message for them. Rufus waited anxiously for Michael's response. He really didn't want to have the ugly reality that his actions may have led directly to the death of his most powerful squad.

Then they heard Michael's exhausted voice through the radio. Rufus's heart pounded with relief as he heard Michael announce in an exhausted but passionate voice,

"Commander Thorne! The job is done, sir!"

* * *

The word spread across the flying fortress and the crew broke out their all their beer and their wine, opening as many bottles and filling up as many glasses as possible so as to celebrate their victory. To the tune of 'See The Conquering Hero, He Comes', Rufus sat down and filled a wine glass.

Pure disbelief gave way to joy as he realised they had just

defeated the Black Mouth. Although he didn't cheer, he raised his glass and he allowed himself to smile. It seemed that he could finally take a rest from his hard taxing work in commanding the war effort now that the Black Mouth, Terra's most formidable enemy, had been finally vanquished.

Jethro then approached him.

"Well...Commander? I don't think there was ever a time before in the whole human race when so many owed their lives to so few. A squad of seven potentially turned the tide of a war which defined the survival of humanity as a species."

"Indeed, Mr Churchill would be proud."

Thinking to himself, Rufus realised there was one more thing to do.

"Come, Colonel Jethro! We must make a visit to our heroes! Heroic work must always be rewarded!"

"We're going down to the ground?"

"Well, I must make eye contact with my men if I'm to maintain their trust in me. Besides, it's about time that I put my feet on the ground." Rufus replied as he placed his peaked cap back on his head.

Jethro smiled as he followed Rufus to the hangar.

* * *

Later that day, Rufus Thorne and Jethro went down in a dropship which touched down on the ground. Surrounded by their comrades, Alpha Squad lined up to attention as Rufus Thorne and his officers approached them. Many of the officers, especially Rufus Thorne himself, were more than glad to finally get their feet on the ground. After having spent so many weeks non-stop in a flying fortress, it was a real pleasure to feel the earth beneath their feet. Rufus locked eyes with Michael.

"So, the Black Mouth is destroyed, Captain?"

"Yes, sir, Zach caused the monster to self-destruct...I told you we would not let you down on, sir!"

Rufus looked away at the remains of the once terrifying

abomination now smouldering in ruin. He turned back to face the squad and asked an officer to bring out the medals.

Rufus surveyed the whole army that had assembled before him. He was now looking into the eyes of all the men he sent to fight and die to secure victory for the human race. It was the first time many of these soldiers had seen Rufus Thorne up close. He was no longer somewhere up on a flying fortress. At that moment, he had come down to look at them all in the eyes like a man.

"Gentlemen!!" He began saying. "A great victory has been won today! Alpha Squad, our finest warriors, have slain the Black Mouth and you have slain the machine armies of the Black Mouth countless times! Mark me, I know the fatigue you all feel! The contempt many of you look at me with. The pain you feel for all the comrades whose death warrants I've signed!! But mark me! I'm as much a man as you all are! I was born into this chaotic world just as you all were! I lament our losses as much as you do!!!"

Zach could see the passion in the voice of Rufus Thorne. He didn't feel as distant as he initially did and spoke with a deep passion and emotion as he continued.

"For I've seen many battles, borne the weight of many defeats and revelled in many victories! The machines can take your life! They can scorch your cities and families as soon as their central command gives them the order! But they can never quash our determination to survive!"

Many of the soldiers were starting to shout out in praise, cheering along as Rufus's voice got louder and more passionate.

"Gentlemen, it has been an honour to serve and fight with you all! You have made Terra proud! Your labour is the reason my uniform glitters with medals bestowed on me by the Terran government!! If you ever feel you need a reason to fight, look not to your money or your statues but to yourselves! You, not the soil, not the buildings, not the vehicles but you and you alone are Terra! Without its people, a nation is nothing but when its people are healthy, proud and alive, it is EVERYTHING!!!"

Cheering erupted from all the men. Rufus Thorne then gave a set of gleaming medals to all of Alpha Squad to congratulate them on their efforts. Zach felt proud but embarrassed when Rufus

Thorne approached him. Zach, who was little more than the son of a barmaid, a new recruit only a week ago, was now face to face with the commander of the Terran army, face to face with a man of genteel origins.

"Was it you, Zach Harker, who slew the Black Mouth?" Throne asked him, sternly.

"Yes, I deactivated it, but I was aided by my comrades and my commander, sir."

Zach shivered with a sense of awe and nervousness as he was face to face with Rufus Thorne. Rufus looked at Zach with pride as he continued.

"Well done, young Harker, you have made all of Terra proud! Your actions will influence our world for many years to come!"

"Thank you, sir."

Zach was about to salute but Rufus saluted him; he saluted the whole army to honour their efforts in keeping humanity safe. In return, they all saluted him. For all his faults, he was their leader and he was as much a Terran as they were.

* * *

When the evening came, the sun began to fall to the ground. The bright glowing moon was starting to soar into the sky, and it illuminated the scenery of the ruined buildings that had been worn by war. Though the buildings looked grim and battered, the people of the city were celebrating their proud victory that they had won. As a result of the celebrations, a city that should otherwise look dead, bland and silent was at that moment vibrant with colour. Squadrons of jets flew overhead in a tight victory parade as part of the celebrations. Fireworks shot out into the sky, bursting into vibrant and colourful shapes before the sparks came down to earth. When they flew past, everyone raised their glasses in praise and delight.

The proud people of Terra drank, partied and feasted all around the world upon learning via news that the Black Mouth had been destroyed. It was one of the finest victories humanity had ever achieved over the machines.

That evening, as he rested outside a bar, Zach looked up and saw the gathered flying fortresses gleaming in the setting sun. He raised his glass of beer in a toast to them for the support that they provided during the battle. Though the Black Mouth was slain, the war would still go on. For the machines were a foe that would never surrender, even if they had no choice. This meant that the chance of Zach ever knowing a time of peace was very slim. Zach wasn't afraid though. He gazed up at a statue of Apollo. The proud masculine figure bore a glowing torch that gleamed throughout the night.

Whatever befell him, and no matter what situation he found himself, one thing was very clear about Zach; he was ready for whatever battle was ahead for him. He was geared for any ordeal that God, Mother Earth, the Machines or even his fellow kinsmen threw at him.

BLOOD AND GEARS LORE

Introduction

Blood and Gears is a novel that takes place in the mid-24th century, but the war that it describes been waged since the last years of the 22nd century. Several questions may arise for the reader as they read this text such as "What is Terra?" and "How all of this begin?" All of this will be explained in the notes that I am about to lay out.

The 2nd Belle Époque

Although the first years of the 21st century were marked by constant instability, perpetual warfare, economic hardship and global pandemics, the second half of the 21st century finally saw a level of stability in which a new form of "Golden age" of science and research took place. One of the most notable breakthroughs was the development of nuclear fusion which allowed a single core to power large cities and vast machines. Two other key developments were the use of hydrogen fuel cells to fuel smaller vehicles such as cars and buses more efficiently but perhaps the most important breakthrough was development of replication plants which could clone materials.

This allowed for an increase in resources which led to the increased production of goods such as houses, cars, lightbulbs and computers. This also meant after a century of facing homelessness and poverty, working class populations across the world could finally afford goods that the more comfortable middle and upper classes had taken for granted. As a result, the standard of living for most of humanity actually began to increase as did the rates of employment and income. At the same time, large leaps were being made in science and research. For example, settlements and colonies were finally being established across the Moon and Mars and even underwater settlements were being established.

Fossil fuels were rendered obsolete by the new forms of energy while leaps had been made in genetic engineering. All forms of new flying vessels which ran on fusion cores and fuel cells and were powered by hover jets became rapidly adapted for a variety of purposes from policing to emergency services to even commercial travel. Devices that lessen the effects of water pressure allowed for larger submarines that could dive deeper, hence allowing underwater settlement and aquaculture. Such settlement would eventually result in the formation of the independent but enigmatic nation of Atlantica. Another key device that was developed in this new age of progress was satellite mounted weather control devices that could alter the weather. Because of this progress, this period was known as "The Second Belle Époque".

However, not everything was utopian during the Second Belle Époque. For example, an attempt to use "weather satellites" by the dawn of the 22nd century to combat rising temperatures resulted in a global cooling in which temperatures began to plummet. The process was stopped by shutting down the satellites but not before temperatures cooled and began a New Ice age. This meant that regions such as the Southern US had temperatures similar to Ireland and Britain while the nations of the Northern hemisphere had to develop underground cities and greenhouses in order to survive the new harsh winters. The new developments of the 2nd Belle Époque also revolutionised warfare which there was still going to be plenty of in the coming centuries.

Pre-World War Three geopolitics
From the late 21st century onwards, the geopolitical situation transformed in a way that couldn't have been easily seen coming. In the wake of Brexit, Britain began to rebuild itself throughout

the 21st century, joining with Canada, Australia and New Zealand to form the "New Commonwealth" or "CANZUK". This nation eventually fused into a single entity called "Greater Albion".

In reaction, France, Germany, Poland and the Scandinavian countries along with other nations came together to form the United States of Europe or USE.

As a result, a new "Irish Question" developed on which entity should Ireland be a part of.

Fatigued of being controlled by a power outside of Ireland, the Republic of Ireland declared itself independent of both powers. As a result, a 2nd Irish civil war broke out between the Albion backed Northern Ireland and the Republic of Ireland which was financially and logistically supported by the USE. Ultimately, the Republican troops, thanks to USE support, won the war and annexed Northern Ireland. This resulted in Ireland being united and becoming a confederation, organised through a dual governance through both Belfast and Dublin. It also resulted in the extreme Unionists forming a diaspora. This new Ireland was able to maintain its independence right up to the outbreak of World War three.

As this was happening, Ukraine joined the USE so as to help prevent yet another Russian invasion of Ukraine, but this resulted in a Cold War between Russia and the USE. As this happened, the US was weakening, mainly due to defeats in the middle East that occurred in the first half of the 21st century, most notably in Afghanistan. Despite no longer being the sole superpower, America was still a robust force. One example of this was when the US was able to support Taiwan against a Chinese invasion. Later when the Chinese tried to seize territory in the Pacific, including Hawaii, both the US and Greater Albion were able to contain Chinese advances in the 2nd Pacific war. Greater Albion joined mainly to defend the sovereignty of Hong Kong.

Meanwhile in the Middle East, the geopolitics had altered thanks to the obsolesce of oil which collapsed the power of groups such as the Saudis and the UAE. In fact, the whole region saw widespread collapse as their oil powered economies increasingly ran out of oil and trading partners. But two major forces survived.

One was Israel which quickly adapted the new technologies and used the new weapons such as flying fortresses, mechs and hover jet dropships to carve out an empire in the Middle East, one that spread as far as Turkey. However, Israel was stopped when it tried to expand into Europe, being stopped by a joint Russian-USE force that managed to grind the Israelis into a stalemate.

The other major power that survived in the Middle East was Egypt. Egypt was able to adapt to the new forms of fuel, mainly hydrogen. But to fuel this new economy, Egypt started programmes to flood the Sahara, partly to gather the water needed but also to fertilize the region for further settlement. While this was successful, it came at the cost of a prolonged war of attrition against the Bedouin nomads who saw the project as a threat to their way of life. This war Egypt was only able to win because of applying its full military might to the region and with support from the Israelis. However, by contrast, Central and South Africa was a completely different scenario...the widespread adoption of replication technology allowed several African countries such as Kenya, Nigeria, the DRC and Zimbabwe to overcome their poverty, allowing their economies to prosper and even allow them to become key powers on the global stage.

South Africa on the other hand soon faced its own crisis due to large scale political corruption and the constant attacks on Boer farms. This resulted in the Boer and other white South Africans splintering off and forming their own new government known as the "New Transvaal". At the same time, the rural communities of South Africa, especially those of Zulu descent, rose up under the leadership of a man who saw himself as a reincarnation of Shaka Zulu who sought to overthrow the weak and corrupt government. The landlocked country of Lesotho did what it could to maintain the civilized order and autonomy as the situation around them deteriorated.

An all-out race war broke out in South Africa and fearing that a potential trade partner could be lost, the Chinese intervened and invaded South Africa. Ironically this new invasion was not well received by the South Africans and forced the whites and blacks to actually team up and drive out the Chinese. Waging a prolonged guerrilla war similar to the "Boer wars", the newly reunited South Africans, supported by America and Greater Albion, managed to defeat the Chinese intervention and restabilize their collapsing republic, creating a new much more stable government which fused with Lesotho. Even the poles became a site of political intrigue as Greater Albion competed with Russia to colonize the Arctic. Greater Albion established a colony in the Arctic that would become another self-governing dominion within its Commonwealth. People from this region would be known as Arcticians.

By the end of the 22nd century after all of this had happened, five major powers dominated world affairs... the USA, the United States of Europe, the Russian federation, the Chinese and Greater Albion. Their continued cold war and arms race meant that World War Three was inevitable.

The Machines
Although the use of fully automated machines for warfare can be traced back even to the use of drones in the late 20th century and early 21st century, it wasn't until the late 21st century that robotic armies started to become common place. Of particular note in this regard were the nations of East Asia. Japan was actually the first nation to truly use robotic armies, partly because they were more efficient but also to keep their economy strong as they had an aging population that was increasingly dwindling. However, the first great power to invest in robotic armies comprised of automated vehicles and robotic soldiers was China. China was still suffering from the consequences of the infamous "One child policy" which meant that even in the late 21st century, China was still having a population crisis. Such a crisis only worsened after the 2nd Pacific war in which most of its conventional army was decimated by the Greater Albion and US forces.

As a result, China by the 22nd century had become the most automated army in the world with only its infantry divisions still being made up of humans. Other major powers such as Russia and the US tried to imitate the Chinese in automating most of their army, but they still used humans for most of their vehicles and aircraft. Although these robots seemed to be more efficient than human armies, they were also much more ruthless. Already the US had problems when a drone would bomb a whole hospital to remove one terrorist. This problem only worsened with the Chinese operation in South Africa in which robotic soldiers would exterminate entire communities of Zulu, Xhosa and even Afrikaners.

This only served to strengthen the backlash that brought those three communities along with others into a single union to fight the Chinese. Despite this, robotic armies continued to be adapted by certain major powers and were used consistently during World War Three. However, this proved to be disastrous because when the US invaded China, the Chinese worked on a secret programme to invent a new robot, one with an organic brain that had the ability to hack enemy robots and turn them against their users. The giant machine would be known as the "Black Mouth" (due to the fact that whenever this machine went, it brought chaos, darkness and blotted out the sun).

The Black Mouth was unleashed and managed to tear through the US invasion of China, repelling it. But then, gradually, it developed a contempt for organic life both animal and human, it believed that synthetic life was superior to organic life, thus turning against humanity as a whole...it hacked the machines of different armies across the world and used them to decimate the human nations they once served. But as Russia, China and the US fell into chaos...two major powers still managed to stand their ground, the question is how?

Legionnaires and meta-human super soldiers

As most of the developed world focused on simply automating their armies, both Greater Albion and the United States of Europe went a different route. While the origin of the Legionnaire programme has mystery around it, what is known is that it started in a sophisticated base in Cornwall known as "Scraw-Fell" where in the middle of the 21st century, the British government took a selection of test subjects, mainly boys between fourteen and twenty-one. Under this project, known as "Project Hercules", the boys were subjected to experiments which augmented their bodies. This involved strengthening their bone structures and their lungs, making their skin thicker and giving their bodies more muscle, not to mention changing the level of adrenaline.

While this made the eldest of the boys strong enough to even lift Britain's light tanks and fling them across the area like a rugby ball, the process was so brutal that it killed the youngest of them, tearing their bodies apart. Enraged by the death of their youngest kinsmen and having been cut off from their families, the surviving boys, led by a nineteen-year-old from Birmingham revolted and managed to almost take over the base of Scraw-Fell, killing normal men and robots twice their size due to their superhuman strength. Only by shutting down the base and using tear gas did the British army manage to contain the boys. Ultimately, they were forced to negotiate with them, allowing them to see their families during each of the key holidays of the year. "Project Hercules" was controversial and it sparked outrage across the world with protests across most cities in Britain, but the opportunity of having a type of soldier which could be even tougher than robots was too much for the New Commonwealth and later Greater Albion to pass over.

At the same time, the USE began its own project "Project Legion" which gathered a number of men between eighteen and thirty from across Europe and sent them to laboratories where they were augmented, trained professionally and formed into regiments.

The New Commonwealth restarted its project using the same approach with better results. Soon, a conference was held in Geneva in regard to how to handle the "Legionnaire question". The leaders of both the USE and the New Commonwealth agreed to set certain rules regarding how the Legionnaires were created and treated.

For example, the augmentation process was restricted to able bodied, physically strong men from eighteen years upwards. (One reason for this was because bodies that are physically weaker than that such as those of boys and girls could be destroyed by the process).

Gradually over time, the Legionnaires began to fill up the ranks of armies such as those of Europe, Greater Albion and even Israel and Ireland. The Legionnaires, though they were often small in number, were notable game changers when it came to battle. (Especially when dealing with terrorists in the Middle East who called them "Nephilim" because of how tough they were). However, in the Pre-World War Three world, the Legionnaires were mainly there to be just special forces, fighter pilots and submariners. Russia even started its own programme coming up to World War Three.

However, during World War three, especially after the revolt of the machines, the USE began to train them in larger numbers. Although the augmentation process was still done at eighteen, the boys in question could be conscripted as young as sixteen to train them beforehand. Soon Europe was able to amass whole armies and divisions comprised of Legionnaires, who manned their own tanks, artillery, ships and flying fortresses. This army though vastly outnumbered by the machines, was able to save Europe, notably making a stand at Warsaw in Poland before pushing them back as far as Western Russia, joining up with the remnants of the Russian army.

Despite this, the attempt to reclaim Moscow was ruined by a counter offensive led by the Black Mouth itself which pushed

Europe's armies in Russia back as far as Saint Petersburg. Though the Europeans managed to save their continent from the fate of the other continents, they were wearied and battered. With surrender not being an option, they turned to the one other superpower that was still standing.

Terra and its origins

While the rest of the world was being torn apart during World War three and then by machine invasions, Greater Albion managed to maintain its strength, mainly thanks to a vast complicated network of naval and aerial assets which defended their mostly island territories from machine attacks.

Only Canada faced a major invasion, but Albionite forces, backed by its Legionnaires and artillery were able to contain the attack. However, though Greater Albion seemed Utopic and impenetrable from the outside, it was being torn apart politically. Perhaps the most notable event in its political history was when Simon, the last prince of Wales, rather than ascending the throne instead abolished the monarchy, turning himself from prince to president and turning Greater Albion into a Republic. Why Simon would do this is yet to be well known but possibly, it was to build on his own dreams of creating unified human power that could defend the species from otherworldly threats. Thus, after the battle of Moscow, Simon sent an Albionite fleet to protect Saint Petersburg from a Machine blockade, preventing the machines from encircling and besieging the battle-hardened but worn-down European army.

Thus, it was during a harsh winter, the Albionite, Russian and European armies held back the machines during a month-long battle. On Christmas Eve, Simon met with the President of the USE, Maximillian, at Paris where they negotiated terms for the future. What resulted was the fusion of the USE and Greater Albion into a new nation known as "Terra" of which Simon was still president with Maximillian as its vice president. Terra became a Federation, a network of self-ruling dominions that answered to a central parliament based in London. Other nations such as Brazil and Ireland joined Terra to repel the machines. The army was reorganized into two factions: The home guard which was a human army that was based on the defence of Terra and the Legion, a meta-human army meant for fighting the machines and reclaiming lost human territory.

One of Terra's most notable achievements was the reclaiming of the USA. For at the dawn of the 23rd century, the US had collapsed into a pattern of feuding warlords who fought both each other while fighting a losing battle against the machines. One such city state, based in Montana, was losing its territory to the machines.

So, its warlord invited the Terrans based in Canada to come into the US to fight the machines. This resulted one of Terra's largest armies launching its invasion of the US. Terra defeated the machines but demanded that the local warlords answer to Terran authority if they were to receive Terran support against the machines. While some warlords accepted Terran rule and as a result became Terran governors and politicians, others resisted the Terran occupation. However, warlord armies were still just humans with rag tag weapons dating from as early as the 21st century. Against the cream of the Terran army, the warlords stood no chance eventually resulting in the whole of North America being controlled by Terran authorities. While this led to North America being redeveloped and stabilized, it also resulted in the forceful confiscation of guns from anyone outside the Terran police and military.

Halfway through the 23rd Century, Terra now controlled Europe, chunks of Africa and South America, Australia and New

Zealand as well as the whole continent of North America. This is the setting for the events of "Blood and Gears".

AUTHOR'S NOTES

Context and origins to novel:

Having first been drafted in 2017 during a holiday in Rome, Blood and Gears is one of the oldest novels that I have written. After years of copy editing, feedback and grammatical proof reading, it is a novel that has evolved a lot from the childish adolescent roots of its genesis. However, the plot of the novel is still substantially the same as it was when first written in 2017: a nineteen-year-old boy from New York, Zach Harker, is press ganged into the Terran military to fight among its genetically augmented super soldier army, known as the Legion, as punishment for what the Terran state deemed murder. He is stationed in Eastern Europe alongside a battle hardened and hostile team of commandos named "Alpha Squad" or "Team Orca." Following a catastrophic defeat at Saint Petersburg, Zach rescues a little Russian boy named Dimitri, whom he sets out to return to his parents, bonding with the squad along the way. After this seemingly small-scale quest is complete, and he and his comrades take on the giant robotic war machine, the Black Mouth.

The first aspect to note about this novel is that it is a text that certain people might find incredibly uncomfortable mainly because of the complex and contradictory nature of Terra, the fictional world government which serves as humanity's final bastion in its war against robotic monsters called "machines." On the one hand, Terra is a republic ruled by elected governments, based in London's Houses of Parliament. It is very much framed within the story as a bastion of civilized morality and human chivalry yet at the same time it has practices that we would consider undemocratic and totalitarian such as press-ganging young men into its "Legion", a genetically augmented army of super soldiers who cannot marry and are there to fight the machines. Terra also executes criminals (especially those who have murdered and raped) instead of simply jailing them which in some views would be extreme.

Zach's situation, an adolescent boy who gets press ganged for killing another youth who had attacked his little brother, is a scenario one can easily imagine happening in dystopian regimes such as the Soviet Union or Oceania, the Anglo spheric government from George Orwell's masterpiece 1984. Yet despite having a mentality that is unapologetically virile and militaristic and behaving in ways that some would consider extreme, Terra is unashamedly in the heroic position that it is ultimately the one force that can substantially defend what remains of humanity from the machines. These machines are unquestionably a monstrous force that want to exterminate what it calls "organic" or living beings.

Thus, all planetary life is as much dependant on Terra's victory as humans are for their survival. To begin with, the first question of Blood and Gears is whether Terra is a nation that is Utopian or Dystopian? The answer is neither. Terra is certainly not a Utopia; it is unashamedly a male centred militaristic nation that is not afraid to flatten its own cities and press gang its own male youth into its army if it wants to. Yet Terra isn't a Dystopia either, for one, it is a nation that does what it can to protect its civilian populace and evacuate them out of harm's way. It is also firmly a multi-cultural and multi-ethnic republic in which individual territories have independent autonomy over their own governance and it is a nation with strong family values as well. The truth is that Terra is a nation state, just like those built by humanity in the Real World. For all of their technological advancements, the Terrans are the same human species as we are, flawed and imperfect and as a result, they suffer from the same flaws as our governments do, such as corruption, class hierarchies and bureaucratic incompetence.

In the real world, some of humanity's greatest nations such as Rome, England and the United States have behaved in ways that were both incredibly heroic and yet have also committed terrible atrocities. Terra, like most nations, has its skeletons in the closet. Yet I do not believe that these flaws in their system should make their stand against the machines any less heroic.

When one considers how dangerous and powerful an artificial intelligence can be in Science Fiction literature, one does have to admire Terra as a civilization for holding its own against such a brutal and terrifying threat which has no interest in diplomacy or coexistence with a form of life that it considers inferior. Perhaps, Terra's totalitarian nature is the product of the violent pressure that is inflicted upon it by warring with violent robots. After all, it wasn't unheard of for democratic nations to engage in practices such as conscription and rationing when under the pressure of invasion. Britain, for example, which is run by an elected Parliament, did both during the two World Wars.

A common flaw I would argue exists in dystopian literature is that it often portrays a society which has no redeeming features and is completely unpleasant to live under. By contrast, Utopian narratives such as Star Trek often portray completely perfect societies with few flaws. Neither image fits the real-life history of a civilization. Civilizations are often as complex and as multi-dimensional as the populace which live within their borders and embody such nation's core ideals. Terra is no different from real life nations, it has traits which make it the pinnacle of civilized ideals to some and a hell on Earth to others.

To understand the mentality of Terra and the key characters of the novel, one has to understand the context that these characters are in, which is of course, the fact that they are fighting a global war against robotic monsters who are much like the Terminator on a grand imperial scale. Blood and Gears can have a rather contradictory message towards warfare for some. Warfare in Blood and Gears is shown in all of its raw brutality and is rife with images that are all too familiar to those who have lived through a war. For in such circumstances, men die young and die horribly on a grand scale, children get orphaned or separated from their parents with a slim chance of seeing them again and the land which you grew to call home is flattened and within an instant, what you knew for most of your life is turned into a chaotic maw that is uninhabitable and unrecognisable. Such scenarios are as familiar to real life contemporary populations such as the Palestinians, Yemeni and Ukrainians as they are to the Terrans in this grim dark future.

The vast and destructive effects of combat between invading non-human monsters and superhuman heroes with advanced and powerful weaponry in highly populated cities is a scenario that has often been turned into a source of popular entertainment by Hollywood (especially in Marvel movies and Godzilla). But it is during such a battle over Saint Petersburg that little Dimitri is separated from his parents and his home is reduced to rubble. Once one peels back the glamorous veneer that Hollywood has built up around combat between meta human beings and monsters, the battle waged between the Terrans and Machines over Saint Petersburg is as destructive and as disruptive as real-life urban combat over cities such as Kabul, Mosul and Kiev. Yet this is not to say that the war in Blood and Gears is not without its heroics. For the Legionnaires, especially our protagonist Zach Harker, are unashamedly heroic.

The final battle against the Black Mouth is ironically a grandiose spectacle straight out of Hollywood with all the epic speeches, descriptions of glamourous combat and great displays of heroics. Thus, Blood and Gears has moments that would not be out of place in an anti-war novel like Under Fire by Henri Barbusse. It also has scenes that would fit perfectly into a marvel superhero film. Just like real life wars, Blood and Gears is comprised of great displays of military heroism and terrible trauma and tragedy.

To tell this story, I drew from numerous genres that I had grown to love as a boy. While Blood and Gears is fundamentally an example of military science fiction, a genre best exemplified by Robert A. Heinlein's Starship Troopers, it also draws on a much more ancient literary tradition: the heroic Epic. Often written in the form of a grand and poetic text that is incredibly long, the heroic Epic told the story of a great man who brought down great beasts, fought valiantly in battle and defended his people, sometimes coming to a tragic end or being undone by his pride.

There are numerous examples of this literary form across many cultures, ranging from the Book of Exodus in the Bible to Homer's Illiad and the Anglo-Saxon poem Beowulf. More modern examples of the Epic narrative would come in the form of John Milton's Paradise Lost and J.R.R. Tolkien's the Lord of the Rings trilogy. The question is, would Blood and Gears fit the definition of an Epic? It is a novel, not a poem, but it tells a grandiose story of horror, bloodshed and glorious combat as within the novel, it is the fate of humanity itself that is at stake.

Central to the epic narrative is the protagonist, who is predominantly what Victorian philosopher Thomas Carlyle called "the Great Man", a mighty male protagonist who achieves greatness by the end of the narrative, becoming the unquestionable hero of his people. Zach is unquestionably that, the hero who fundamentally brings down the "Black Mouth" and is recognised as a hero in the eyes of the Terran people.

But Zach doesn't start out a "great man," he starts out as an unhappy boy who lost his father to a robotic bombardment when he was nine, leaving his mother to raise him and his younger brother Phil alone. At nineteen, he is forced into the army, not because of any divine call, but to escape the death penalty. Through a stubborn determination to soldier on, Zach overcomes brutal ordeals with the help of his comrades and ultimately takes on the Black Mouth. In many ways, Zach plays the triple role that shapes a man of war, at various points of his life, he is a conqueror, hero and victim all in one. For like many children throughout history, he lost a parent and got robbed of a happy childhood because of war.

Like many men, he was forced into the army, his freedom

being the cost of upholding the stability of his nation. Yet ironically, he becomes to be seen by Terrans in the same light that Alfred the Great or the Duke of Wellington would be seen by the English: the image of a Great Man. In some ways, Zach could be seen as an "everyman" in the context of war, for at least some aspects of his character, be it the traumatised child, the conscripted youth or the great leader of men, has been the experience of real-life men in a time of war.

It is worth noting that Zach is only introduced in the fourth chapter. The role of the first three chapters is to set up the team that Zach is to serve alongside so that one gets a good insight into their mentality before he joins them, what happened to them and why Zach is being added to their squad. Of central focus in these early chapters, is Zach's commander, Michael, framed as the Byronic hero and essentially the "father wolf" of the team. He is experienced where Zach is new, he is harsh and stoic where Zach is warm and emotional, he is regimented where Zach is rebellious. Yet at heart, both men are unquestionably heroic and as a result, they are a mirror image of each other. Zach is what Michael once was while Michael is what Zach will probably become if he survives.

This is quite a common tactic in literature, to spend the early chapters of a book setting up the supporting characters before introducing a main protagonist. For example, the first few chapters of Madame Bovary by Flaubert focus on Emma Bovary's husband Charles and she is not introduced until much later. Similarly in Tom Clancy's The Hunt for Red October, Jack Ryan is not introduced until later chapters with the first chunk of the book focusing on the mutinous Lithuanian captain Marco Ramius. Thus, Blood and Gears does the same technique, setting up the key supporting characters from which the protagonist will be measured against.

While Zach foils and mirrors against many characters, perhaps one of the most notable and important characters of the novel is the Terran Grand Marshall, Commander Rufus Thorne, who more than any other character in Blood and Gears embodies the contradictions and complexity at the heart of the Terran State.

On one hand, Rufus Thorne is a cold, stoic and ruthless commander who would flatten a whole city if he were going to lose it to the machines. The logic being that the enemy would not be able to use its capacities for future operations.

Positioned within the security of a flying fortress, (a giant flying machine that functions both as a battleship and aircraft carrier for the Terrans), Rufus can be firmly read as an armchair general who sends men to their death, literally disconnected from the pain that his actions often inflict. Much like the generals in poetry of the First World War, he comes off as a disconnected figure in the eyes of the main squad. However, Rufus himself is painfully aware of the humanity he has had to sacrifice in order to maintain the security of the Terran state. Most notably in his speech to Colonel Jethro, his more emotionally empathetic counterpart, Rufus firmly decrees that the cost of civilization is the "blood of men" as he puts it.

Whether he is simply acknowledging the brute reality that there is a human cost to securing a nation's freedom and its existence in the face of chaos or simply an attempt to rationalize and justify the nastier actions he has ordered is something I will leave up to the reader. Part of what makes Rufus Thorne uncomfortable is that he does not say what we want to hear. He does not give words of comfort or warmth the way one's parents, especially one's mother would give us. He does not take a little boy under his wing the way Zach does, nor does he evoke the wise but firm fatherly image that Michael Faulkner does...but rather, Rufus tells the brute truth. The brute reality of life is that no matter how technologically advanced or politically complicated our society becomes, men often died to preserve it, especially in times of warfare like the First and Second World War or even the Irish War of Independence and American Civil War. But also in accidents, such as on the HMS Birkenhead in which the soldiers stayed behind so that their wives and children could get on the boats or the so called "bio robots", conscripted young men who cleaned up the irradiated rubble after the Chernobyl accident in hope of containing the radioactive spread.

Thus Rufus, as blunt and as brutal as he is, tells an uncomfortable truth that we don't like to hear. It may not justify his scorched earth policies or his apathy in the eyes of readers but it does explain the way he thinks about the world.

He is fighting a war after all, and war has often forced political and military leaders to make uncomfortable decisions. This is not to say that Rufus doesn't have his humanity, he certainly does. For example, when he is about to flatten Saint Petersburg, Rufus Thorne orders the evacuation of Saint Petersburg. Just like real life exoduses such as Dunkirk and the fall of Kabul, such an evacuation ends up being chaotic but it does ensure that Saint Petersburg's population survives. In real life such as in Dresden, cities were bombed and destroyed without concern for the civilian population. On that front, Rufus shows a fair bit more humanity and compassion for the local populace than other political and military leaders have done. Like the rest of the characters, Rufus would wish for nothing more than the end of the war, and he knows all too well that the one way to end the war is to win it.

It is going to be brutal; it is going to be costly; it will have many nightmarish experiences for those involved but it is going to have to be won if humanity is to survive.

Of final note to this introduction is of course the antagonist to Blood and Gears, the Black Mouth, the central AI that is in charge of the machines. I got the name "the Black Mouth" from a children's movie called the Little Polar Bear which involves a giant robotic ship which consumes the arctic creatures and is called "the Black Mouth." Though on surface level, the Black Mouth seems like a very one-dimensional antagonist, a giant crab shaped war machine that seeks to destroy humanity, it was originally built to defend China from American invasion during the Third World War only to turn on humanity later on. The Black Mouth is ultimately a force of industrial might robbed of any civilized virtue or religious ethics that would govern a human society.

This could easily apply to the machines as a whole, they were programmed to kill and that is what they are doing.

Purely metallic without any advanced cognitive thought or empathy, the machines think in very simple terms with the Black Mouth being the only proper AI, an AI filled with rage against humanity. The machines have no real sense of individuality or character that humans do because they are simplistic synesthetic creations of the military industrial complex. Legionnaires, despite being genetically augmented, display complex human emotions from empathy to anger to a longing for home and thus are able to be more than just mindless killers, a one-dimensional mentality that the machines are just trapped in.

To conclude, Blood and Gears is an uncanny epic in which each character and faction is a lot more complicated than what they seem.

ABOUT THE AUTHOR

Declan Cosson

Declan Cosson was born in Paris, France in 1999. He moved to Ireland in 2001 where he has lived ever since.
He attended Hollypark school between 2005 and 2012. He then attended Clonkeen College between 2012 and 2018 and studied English, Media and Cultural Studies in IADT in Dun Laoghaire between 2018 and 2022.

Declan started writing as early as fifteen years old and has been writing ever since. Currently he is 23 years old. During his time in Clonkeen, he contributed short stories to the Clonkeen Anthology and also contributed short stories to Ink slinger's anthology at the Irish Writer's centre. In 2021, he published a short story collection called the "Collection of the Yearly Strange". "Blood and Gears" is Declan Cosson's latest work.

BOOKS BY THIS AUTHOR

Collection Of The Yearly Strange

The Collection of the Yearly Strange is a short story collection that details terrifying encounters throughout history into the future. These tales will take you from the gas lit streets of early 20th century London to the Mid-Western US at the height of the Cold War and then towards the deepest depths of the Atlantic Ocean and even to the furthest reaches of the Alpha Centauri. Along the way, you will meet a plethora of creatures ranging from heroic humans to robotic and insectoid monstrosities to even alien invaders ready to abduct. Though the tools, culture and weapons may change throughout history, one constant in these tales remains. And that is that there is always something that goes bump in the night when you least expect it. Because of that these tales are not for the faint hearted.

ACKNOWLEDGEMENT

I would like to thank everyone, especially my family who has supported me in the completion and publication of my book. I would particularly like to thank Jeremy Murphy and his agency for giving the much needed guidance and support in publishing my novel.

Finally, I would like to thank the Inkslingers from the Irish Writers center for their support and advice when it comes not just to publishing this novel, but the novels that are to come.